RAVENSPIRE

RAVENSPIRE

•

Marilyn Prather

AVALON BOOKS
THOMAS BOUREGY AND COMPANY, INC.
401 LAFAYETTE STREET
NEW YORK, NEW YORK 10003

Fic
PRA

© Copyright 1998 by Marilyn Prather
Library of Congress Catalog Card Number 97-97217
ISBN 0-8034-9287-1
All rights reserved.
All the characters in this book are fictitious,
and any resemblance to actual persons,
living or dead, is purely coincidental.

PRINTED IN THE UNITED STATES OF AMERICA
ON ACID-FREE PAPER
BY HADDON CRAFTSMEN, BLOOMSBURG, PENNSYLVANIA

For Matthew and Lynn Gaige,
whose friendship I treasure

and

For John, Bente and Shane Esquibel,
in loving memory of Bianca

Chapter One

Andrea Lane buttoned her coat against the dank, chill air and crossed the expanse of lawn that separated the Seacliff Inn from The Timbers Café. Heavy clouds banked the sky above, and mist draped the pine-forested hills to the east like a delicate veil.

The weather in Seacliff, Washington, was a marked contrast to the oppressive heat and hazy sunshine Andrea had left behind in Boston. When she'd boarded the plane that morning, the pollution that hung over the city like a curtain dulled the cast of the sky, turning it a dirty shade of blue.

Andrea much preferred a gentle shower of rain to haze; low, verdant mountains to glass-domed skyscrapers. And she preferred air so clear her lungs felt cleansed when she drew in a breath of it. Still, she chided herself for neglecting to bring anything more substantial than a sweater or her raincoat for protection against the elements. Her memories of summers spent with her grandmother—Nanna, as she'd fondly called the silver-haired woman—should have served her better, even if those summers seemed distant to her now, and her memories of them were tinged with a certain feeling of sadness.

She shoved her hands in her pockets for warmth. In the left pocket her hand made contact with a paperback that she'd forgotten she'd stashed there. A favorite Agatha Christie or Ellery Queen mystery, no doubt. In the other pocket, her fingers closed around a piece of paper on which was drawn a map. That piece of paper had become a sort of worry stone for her over the past weeks.

Whenever she'd begun to feel anxious about her trip and

its purpose, she would pull out the map and the letter from the Manning Employment Agency, which were stored in her purse. She would reread the letter that informed her of the interview the agency had arranged for her. Then she'd study the map, with its curving lines and arrows and the note dashed across the bottom of the page. *I hope my directions aren't confusing,* the note read. It was signed *Holt Carraday.* A telephone number was scrawled at the bottom.

Andrea smiled to herself. More than once she'd been tempted to phone Mr. Holt Carraday and inform him that his directions *were* confusing. But she'd resisted, though she had to admit she was curious about the looks and disposition of the man who'd drawn those bold lines and arrows. She trusted that she would be able to make sense of his instructions when the time came to follow them.

That time was drawing near, and Andrea unconsciously quickened her pace until she reached the small restaurant tucked between rows of stately red cedar trees.

The inside of The Timbers Café was cheery—and warm, Andrea discovered as she stepped through the door. Electric hurricane lamps cast a bright, flickering glow over the room crammed with tables and booths, all of which were vacant at the moment. The walls, festooned with colorful buoys and fish netting and pictures of lighthouses, conveyed a nautical theme.

The decor reflected the environment of the area. From what she'd been able to learn about Seacliff, Andrea knew that the village's economy was tied to the local fishing industry. Approaching Seacliff from the south, she'd spotted a sign at the side of the road bearing the words *Washington Coast Cannery* and caught a glimpse through the trees of a large brick building. Her nose had picked up a slight fishy odor as she passed the cannery, but she'd imagined too that she'd detected the faint tangy smell of the sea and heard the roar of waves pounding on stone. She hoped that soon she would be able to draw that salty scent into her nostrils and watch the ocean's great foamy waves break on a rocky shore.

It'll be like when Nanna was alive.

No, a tiny voice thrummed inside Andrea's head. *It can never be like that again.* A shiver passed through her, and she pressed the collar of her coat closer to her neck.

"A table or a booth?"

The question cut into Andrea's thoughts, and she turned to find a plump, gray-haired woman standing beside her. The woman wore a crisp white apron—and an inquisitive expression on her round, matronly face.

"A booth, please."

The waitress showed Andrea to a booth with a window view of the café's parking lot.

"Are you staying at the inn?"

Andrea saw only a blurry image when she looked at the waitress, and she realized that her glasses must have fogged up. She usually wore contact lenses. But today her eyes had felt gritty and tired from lack of sleep, and she'd decided that the black-framed glasses would be a more comfortable choice than her contacts.

"Miss?"

In her preoccupation with the glasses, Andrea realized she hadn't answered the waitress's question. "Yes, I'm staying at the motel." She cleaned the glasses with a napkin and put them back on.

The waitress leaned closer. "Just call me Maggie." She pointed at the name tag pinned to her blouse. "You're here on business, I suppose. Something to do with the cannery, I'll bet. An article in the paper just yesterday said the building is up for sale."

Though she could have been irritated by Maggie's nosiness, Andrea found herself smiling. The waitress possessed a motherly air that appealed to her.

"No, Maggie, I'm not here on business." She paused. "Well, I guess you could say that I am," she amended. "I'm a teacher and I'm here for a job interview."

Maggie's bushy eyebrows arched. "A teacher. I should've known."

"Why should you have known?"

"Because you're the..." She shook her head and gazed toward the ceiling while she counted on her fingers. "The fourth one in six months." Her eyes met Andrea's again. "You're having an interview with Mr. Carraday, I'd wager. Out at that mansion. It's off the scenic highway—off the beaten path, in fact."

"Yes, I'm having an interview with Mr. Carraday."

Maggie frowned and chewed briefly on her lower lip. "None of the other young women lasted, it seems." She retrieved a menu from a nearby table and plopped it down in front of Andrea.

Andrea opened the menu and stared at it for a moment without seeing anything that was printed there. Finally, she returned her attention to the waitress. "Are you saying that Mr. Carraday hired three different tutors for his daughter in the past six months?"

"That's what I'm saying. All of them stayed at the inn. And all of them left Mr. Carraday within a month to the day of being hired. Can't say as I blame them."

"Why wouldn't you blame them?" Was Maggie trying to hint that Mr. Carraday's daughter, Elizabeth, was something of a terror?

"Dear, who could possibly fault them for wanting to get away from that spooky old mansion of his as soon as possible?"

Andrea sat up straighter. Spooky old mansion? All the Manning Agency had told her about Holt Carraday was that he was a widower who owned a small pharmaceutical company and an estate called Ravenspire. And that he had an eight-year-old daughter who was in need of a tutor and that the tutor would be given room and board in addition to her salary. "You think they were afraid to live there?"

Maggie looked speculative. "I certainly would have been if I were in their shoes. But I've got my own notion as to why they left in such a hurry."

Andrea paused a heartbeat. "What's that, Maggie?"

"They were all too pretty." The waitress's voice was low, almost whispery. "And *he* let them go."

Pretty. How long had it been since anyone had called Andrea that? Her hand automatically sought the uneven scar that ran from the top of her right ear to her jawline. She missed part of Maggie's next words.

"... Holt Carraday being a good-looking man and all, I expect the temptation would be great for him to..." Her words trailed off.

The implication wasn't lost on Andrea. "You believe he was attracted to the other tutors?"

"Just my own idea, dear. Word is that, except for his business travels, the man has kept to himself, holed up like a hermit since his wife's death. Used to be they hosted grand parties nearly every weekend. Always people coming and going—all wealthy, mind you, and some of them famous. The parties were *her* doing, everyone says. Now the man lives in isolation. But Holt Carraday *is* a man, isn't he?" Maggie chattered on. "And a man has certain... needs, don't you know. You were aware that he lost his wife a few years back?"

"I was told he's a widower," Andrea said.

Maggie leaned closer. "But you weren't told how his wife died, were you?"

Andrea shook her head, not sure that she wanted to know.

"Victoria Carraday was a beautiful woman, dear. They say the child's the picture of her. Anyway, it was no secret that she'd been a stage actress—and deeply involved with a famous actor before her marriage. Twice her age, he was." Maggie clucked softly. "Rumor is that she never got over him—even after her marriage to Mr. Carraday. Pity, though, that she fell into the ocean. A terrible accident, according to our local sheriff. Lost her footing, he said."

A chill edged up Andrea's spine. "Mr. Carraday must have been devastated by his wife's death."

Maggie shrugged. "Hard to say. He was off somewhere on business at the time. The tabloids had a field day, I tell you. Write-ups about the Carradays' loveless marriage and speculation about suicide. Folks have taken their lives for lesser reasons than . . . You might work out though,'' Maggie went on more cheerfully. "With those glasses and your red hair pulled back in that no-nonsense style, I'd bet my new Sunday dress that he'll keep you on if he hires you. Providing you've decided that you want to work for him.''

And if I don't mind living in that spooky old mansion of his and dealing with the idea that his wife fell—or jumped— to her death in the ocean. Andrea looked away.

Maggie was only trying to be helpful, she told herself. And if she was hinting that Andrea was plain, it was nothing but the truth. Though Andrea usually wore her long, naturally curly hair loose around her shoulders, for the trip she'd fastened it back with decorative barrettes, and she'd chosen her unadorned navy linen suit and white blouse as the most appropriate attire she owned for an interview. She had kept her makeup simple, too, just foundation and the concealer that she always wore to hide the scar, plus a bit of blush and a hint of lipstick.

Meeting Maggie's gaze, she saw that the waitress's cheeks were flushed, and she wondered if Maggie were embarrassed. Andrea cast about for something to say. "I appreciate . . ." she began, intent on letting Maggie know she didn't fear what she might find at Ravenspire.

Suddenly, a man's coarse voice boomed out Maggie's name from the rear of the café.

Maggie gave a startled cry and whirled around. Her ample hips collided with the table and sent the menu sailing toward the floor. The waitress caught the menu in midair. "I'm sorry," she gasped, nervously edging the menu into Andrea's hands. "That's the cook calling. He's got a nasty temper, and he'll report me to Charlie if I don't get my salads made. Charlie's the owner." She whipped out an order pad from her apron pocket. "What can I get you, dear?"

Andrea's mind was anywhere but on food. She pointed randomly at the menu. "This," she said without looking down. It wasn't until the waitress had bustled off to the kitchen that Andrea read what she had ordered. When she saw it was the breaded veal cutlet platter, she made a show of distaste, though there wasn't anyone around to notice. She detested veal, rarely ate meat that was breaded and fried. But it hardly mattered. After what Maggie had told her, she had no appetite anyway.

At a bend in the highway about ten miles out of Seacliff, Andrea spotted a rest stop. She swung her leased Honda onto the paved driveway and pulled up beside a picnic table. Shortly after she'd left the inn, her left calf had developed a cramp for some reason, and she decided the stop would give her a chance to stretch her legs.

Besides, she'd begun the trip with an uptight feeling that had increased as she got closer to Ravenspire. One of the problems was that she'd been replaying the conversation between herself and the waitress over and over in her head. Maggie's comments about Holt Carraday and the succession of tutors that had come and gone from Ravenspire—not to mention her revelations about his wife's death—had raised more than a few disturbing questions in Andrea's mind. She desperately needed to keep her head clear of any notions she might be tempted to form about her prospective employer if she hoped to have a productive interview with him.

Andrea neatly folded her coat on the passenger seat and got out of the car. When her gaze wandered to the picnic table, she saw that it was littered with the decaying remains of someone's meal. Beer bottles and soda cans were strewn in the grass at the base of the table while, nearby, a trash can sat empty.

"Look at this, Andy," her grandmother would have said if she were here. *"Just goes to prove how selfish some folks are, how they spoil things for others."*

Andrea turned away from the table in disgust and let her eyes drink in the sight of the Pacific spread out to the brink of the wide horizon. Gray-green waves rode in under a lowering sky. Andrea admired the ocean's majesty as its white crests broke with a muffled roar over the rocks below. *"Now that,"* Nanna would have told her with a sweep of her weathered hand, *"is proof of a far greater and wiser power."*

Andrea smiled to herself. She was here, on the coast that her grandmother had so loved. There was nothing to fear. She drew in deep refreshing breaths of the salt-scented air as she walked back and forth across the parking area. The cramp in her leg eased, and the knot in her stomach began to unravel. Her mind cleared, too, turning to a more positive train of thought.

Who cared if the tabloids had enjoyed a field day with speculation over the Carradays' marriage and the possibility that Victoria's death was intentional instead of accidental? Andrea tried to push the thought from her head. She never bought the tabloids or read them. And as for the town busybodies and their idle rumors about the circumstances surrounding the tragedy, hadn't Maggie herself admitted that Seacliff was a small town and its citizens liked to gossip? Then there was the waitress's notion that Holt Carraday lived in a spooky old mansion. Maybe that was just Maggie's perception of the place. The house couldn't really be *that* bad, could it?

With a sigh and a last look back at the water, Andrea walked over to the picnic table, gathered up the trash, and deposited it in the barrel.

Returning to her car, she sat for a moment, examining her image in the vanity mirror. Had she applied enough concealer? No matter how much she used, she knew the scar could never be completely hidden from inquisitive eyes. To be safe, Andrea tugged loose a few strands of hair and smoothed them over the scar as best she could. Then, after consulting Mr. Carraday's map for a final time, she drove off.

There was almost no traffic on the highway, which angled sharply inland for several miles—just as the hand-drawn map had indicated—then wound back again to hug the coastline. With the knowledge that every bend in the highway was bringing her nearer to her destination, Andrea grew more alert. A heightened sense of anticipation set her nerves on edge.

At last Andrea spied the sign she'd been watching for, and she slowed the Honda to a crawl. One word, written in bold black letters, stood out against the gray background of the sign. "Ravenspire," Andrea read under her breath. Her heart gave a lurch. On top of the sign sat the uncanny likeness of a raven, its wings outstretched and its head pointed toward the Pacific.

On the other side of the sign was a lane, flanked on either side by bigleaf maple trees, their leaves already faded from their autumn hues of red and gold to drab brown. Gripping the steering wheel tighter, Andrea turned onto the lane. The twisted branches of the trees with their dying leaves formed a ghostly arch over the drive, like a grim welcoming committee whose dark, gnarled arms reached out to enfold her. Finally, the way opened up and she got her first glimpse of Ravenspire.

She supposed the vast and rambling structure spread before her in the midst of a lawn of towering trees and beds of grass could be termed a "house." The waitress had called it a mansion. The word "castle" sprang to Andrea's mind, as she gazed in awe at Ravenspire's rough-hewn walls. Their uneven gray stones looked as if they'd been hauled from the ocean and flung down in this desolate place where some giant's hand had barely succeeded in piecing them together and chiseling out their windows and columns and parapets. Perhaps, she thought, that was how Gossington Hall looked—the castle where Miss Marple solved the mystery of *The Body in the Library*.

But this was no novel, she told herself. This was real life, and Ravenspire was no ordinary home. Maggie had said that Holt Carraday lived like a hermit. The high walls of Ravenspire certainly hinted at the possibility. After all, how many wealthy men lived in castles these days?

Her anxious gaze was drawn to the tower that anchored

the mansion's westernmost corner. The tower jutted skyward, its top reaching higher than the rest of the home. Fingers of fog curled around the spire and snaked, phantomlike, down its sides. The few windows in the tower were dark, and the mansion appeared deserted, as if its occupants had abandoned it long ago without any plans to return.

Andrea shuddered, her determination to keep an upbeat attitude about Holt Carraday and the impending job interview vanishing as fast as the waning daylight. Should she just drive off? Her inherent stubborn streak quickly overcame her cowardice. She hadn't traveled three thousand miles to turn and run like a frightened rabbit without at least meeting the man who owned Ravenspire. Before she could change her mind again, she parked the Honda and walked briskly up to the imposing front door.

The door, of some dark, rich-grained wood, sported carvings of sailing vessels. Andrea admired the carvings briefly as she pressed the doorbell. She heard the distant sound of chimes, and soon the door swung open. On the other side stood a fair-haired woman, small-boned and slender, with a forgettable yet pleasant face. Andrea assumed the woman was Mr. Carraday's housekeeper, but she looked almost laughably out of her element standing there on the threshold, dwarfed by the size and magnificence of the door and the home behind it.

"Miss Lane?" the woman inquired softly. "Won't you come in?"

Andrea stepped into a huge foyer paneled in wood the same color and texture as the door. The foyer impressed Andrea as shadowy, filled with mysterious recesses and dark corners. A pair of brass floor lamps provided the only illumination, and their anemic pools of light served to enhance the dreary aura of the room.

With an indrawn breath of anticipation, Andrea glanced around, half expecting to find crossed swords and bucklers on the drab walls or a rusted suit of armor standing silent guard in one of those secret recesses. But she saw no swords

Ravenspire 11

or bucklers or suits of armor, only a bouquet of mixed flowers past their prime bowing their heads over the side of a squat vase on an occasional table, and a couple of paintings of Ravenspire gracing one of the walls.

"Mr. Carraday will see you in his study, Miss Lane." The housekeeper's thin voice echoed weakly off the walls. "If you'll come with me." She raised her hand in a brief gesture.

Andrea noted that two corridors led off the foyer, one to the right, the other to the left. The housekeeper turned toward the left hallway, and Andrea followed. The ceiling of the corridor was arched, like the ceiling of a stately cathedral, and along the walls, disproportionately small torch lamps lent their dim, wavering glow to the polished flagstone floor.

Was Mr. Carraday trying to save on his electric bills? Andrea smiled at her own grim joke. But she had been right about one thing. Ravenspire was a castle—of sorts.

Utter quiet dominated the passageway, and all the doors that Andrea passed by were shut tight, hiding whatever lay behind them. Only the last door on the right showed any sign of life. A light spilled through the open door into the corridor, throwing distorted shadows over the floor and wall.

The housekeeper came to a stop at the open door. "In here," she said, turning to Andrea with a slight smile. "Please take a chair by the desk. Mr. Carraday will be with you shortly."

Andrea watched as the housekeeper turned and walked back down the corridor. She wasn't sure if she should be relieved or upset that Holt Carraday wasn't on hand to greet her. But when she stepped across the threshold and into the study, she observed that the room was a bit less dismal and tomblike than the foyer and hallway, and she decided that having a few moments alone was to her advantage. She would have a chance to compose her thoughts.

The study projected a lived-in look, if not a cozy one. The room was well lit by a number of lamps and two French windows that, on a clear day, would draw in plenty of sunshine. At the same time, Andrea was keenly aware of the unmistakable masculine air that pervaded the room and its furnishings.

A man's influence was reflected in the massive rock fireplace that took up most of one wall of the study. It was evident, too, in the choice of furniture, from the floor-to-ceiling bookcases filled with books that occupied a corner of the room to the handsome desk of carved oak that held court near the center. Behind the desk stood a worn-looking black leather chair—the type Andrea imagined an astute businessman would choose to sit in. A smaller Edwardian-style chair, upholstered in a rich plaid fabric, was set near the front of the desk.

But it wasn't the fireplace or the furniture that captured Andrea's interest. It was the room's decor. The walls were covered with paintings of ships, and miniatures of the vessels, each housed in its own glass display case, crowded every available table and nook and cranny of the study. Andrea had a sudden vision of Mr. Carraday striding into the room like a sort of modern-day Captain Ahab.

Well, she wasn't quite ready to mutiny yet—not until she saw the man, at least. *Does he harbor a secret wish to be a sailor?* she wondered, picking up one of the smaller cases and inspecting the tiny ship housed inside. Or, like her, was he simply fascinated by anything having to do with the sea? The ship was constructed of polished wood, she observed, its riggings and sails so authentic-looking that it was easy to imagine them billowing and flapping as the tiny ship tacked against a make-believe wind.

Had Mr. Carraday constructed all of the model ships that decorated his study? Whoever had pieced them together must have had infinite patience for the task.

From somewhere behind Andrea a clock chimed out, and she turned with the case still in her hands. In the center of the marble mantel stood an ornate gold-framed clock. Gingerly putting the case back where she'd found it, Andrea crossed the room to check her watch against the clock. The timepieces were in harmony. That meant Mr. Carraday was a good ten minutes late for the appointed interview. Unlike a builder of model ships, she had little patience—at least when she was kept waiting.

Andrea began to pace, a habit she had when she was perturbed. She walked back and forth across the room, pausing briefly to debate whether or not she should sit down in the upholstered chair. But her nerves were wound too tight for her to sit placidly until Holt Carraday decided to make his entrance. So she went back to pacing.

At one end of the room, Andrea slowed her steps to stare absently at a painting; at the other end, she inspected, almost without seeing, another miniature imprisoned in glass. She came to a full stop once, in front of the hearth. A gray mound of dead ashes gave evidence of some long-extinguished fire, and a chill swept through Andrea as she tried to picture the hearth on a winter's night, heaped with a pile of burning logs, crackling with light and warmth. But from the looks of it, a fire hadn't been laid in the hearth for a good while.

Suddenly, the tick of the clock seemed to be louder; the passing of each second, each minute, lengthened into hours in Andrea's mind. But another glance at her watch showed that only another ten minutes had gone by. With a quick gesture, she pushed up her glasses, which had slid down her nose.

Why had Mr. Carraday kept her waiting? Was he one of those egotistical types who assumed that sauntering in late for an appointment served to magnify his importance?

Pivoting on her heel, Andrea marched over to the largest and most impressive painting in the room. With feigned concentration, she studied the portrait of the magnificent sailing ship that was set in the midst of a turbulent sea. Beneath a sky black with the clouds of an approaching storm, great frothy waves poured over the leaning hull of the vessel whose sails were banked against the wind. Andrea's gaze slipped lower, and she spied something engraved on a gold plaque at the base of the painting. She leaned closer to make out the words.

"Tragically, Miss Lane, the *Royal Charles* was captured by the Dutch in a fiercely fought battle and towed off to Holland a broken vessel."

Chapter Two

Andrea gasped at the sound of the husky male voice. Whirling around, she faced a tall, dark-haired man. He stood in the doorway, one hand resting against the jamb.

"The year was 1665," he said. He withdrew his hand and headed toward her.

Andrea's attention was no longer on paintings of ships or their models, but on the man whose long strides ate up the distance between the two of them. *"Holt Carraday being a good-looking man and all,"* Maggie had said.

The waitress's words were a woefully inadequate estimation of the vision of masculinity that came to a stop in front of Andrea. With his black, roughly curled hair and ruggedly sculpted features, Holt Carraday was devastatingly handsome.

A black suede jacket, loosely buttoned, spanned his broad shoulders. Underneath the jacket, an ivory sweater fit snugly against his chest, and gray slacks emphasized the long line of his legs.

His appearance held no resemblance at all to the swarthy sea captain Andrea had imagined a moment ago. Nor did he look like a hermit. Instead, he could have stepped off the pages of *GQ*. Or in another lifetime, he might have been a nobleman, a sultan, a prince whose kingdom was called Ravenspire. Andrea grew uncomfortably warm at the fanciful thought, and she began to look away from the man who might soon be her employer.

But Holt Carraday's gaze caught hers, and she was forced to meet his eyes. They were startlingly clear and icy blue, like agates bathed in the cold waters of the Pacific. Andrea had never seen eyes like his before, and in that instant she knew that this man would never bend to another's orders or wishes. He was someone who—hermit or no—knew how to command authority whenever circumstances warranted it.

"I've kept you waiting," the "nobleman" said after an interminable pause.

No apology followed, and Andrea doubted Holt Carraday ever apologized for anything he did. But her irritation at him was now buried under a dozen other emotions, none of which she could define, and so she offered him her hand and a forced smile. "I'm pleased to meet you, Mr. Carraday."

His firm, full mouth twitched at the corners, as if it might break into a smile. But Holt Carraday didn't smile, though his hand took hers in a confident grip; his fingers, smooth and tapered and strong, wrapped around her much smaller ones. An odd tingling coursed through Andrea where his hand had held hers.

He moved ahead of her to take the leather chair. "Won't you have a seat." He gestured toward the upholstered chair.

Andrea averted her eyes from his cold blue stare. She sat down, taking undue care to smooth her skirt over her knees. All the while she sensed that he was watching her. Was this how it was for all the other women who came to work for him?

As if by design, Andrea's glasses slipped down her nose again. She pushed them up with a hasty jerk that caused them to dig painfully into the bridge of her nose.

"I hope you didn't have any trouble following my map." He took a folder from the top drawer of his desk and laid it open in front of him.

Heat flooded Andrea's cheeks as she cast a glance at the man who sat across from her. "It was . . . readable," she said.

"Good."

Under his scrutiny, Andrea grew more uncomfortable by the minute. It wasn't just the notion that she found him unsettlingly attractive. She began to wonder if he had noticed the scar. She knew how a person's eyes could be drawn to it, how one could stare at it without meaning to. Lifting her chin, she met his eyes directly and saw that he didn't appear to be staring at the scar, after all. Before she could figure out what it was about her that had aroused his curiosity, he bowed his head over the folder and began to shuffle through the papers in it.

"I see from your résumé that you were employed at a private school in Boston for the past three years." He lifted a sheet of paper from the folder.

Andrea straightened. She rested her hands carefully on the arms of the chair. "Yes. I taught a combined third- and fourth-grade class at Bayard Academy."

He studied the sheet of paper for what seemed an eternity. "I understand the school closed not long ago," he said, raising his eyes.

Andrea nodded, too aware of the arresting quality of his gaze. "Last spring." Though she'd been shocked by the news at the time, she had come to the conclusion that the closing was for the best in her case. "The campus in Boston was a branch of the original school in Maine. The trustees decided that the academy's—and the students'—interests would be better served by consolidating the two campuses into one."

"That meant you and the rest of the faculty in Boston were left without jobs."

"We were given the option of transferring to the other campus, but I declined." That option was still open to her, she told herself. The superintendent and trustees had made it clear that she would be welcome back any time.

Mr. Carraday folded his hands together. "Why are you interested in finding employment on the other side of the country, Miss Lane?" He leaned forward. "And tell me why I should hire you as my daughter's tutor."

All the rehearsed answers she'd formed in her mind suddenly froze in her throat. But her voice sounded calm enough when she replied, "I believe my three years of experience at the academy have prepared me well for giving private instruction and for relating one-on-one with a student." She paused, collecting her thoughts. "Classes at the academy were generally limited to a maximum of seven or eight students per instructor. That meant I had the chance to get to know each of my pupils and tailor the lessons to his or her needs."

Mr. Carraday acknowledged her with a nod of his head. "You taught all the basic?"

"Yes. Math, reading and grammar, science, history, every subject except for music."

"Well, from your résumé I can see that your qualifications are excellent." He snatched a second sheet of paper from the folder and examined it. "You gave riding instruction, too?"

"That's right, but only during the summers. There were stables, tennis courts, and a swimming pool at the Maine campus. Every year, the students from the Boston campus would attend summer camp in Maine. I gave riding lessons and conducted workshops."

"Interesting." Those impassive eyes were studying her again. "But you still haven't answered my first question. Why do you want to teach here, where the nearest city of any size is a good eighty miles away?"

Andrea swallowed back the sudden lump that had come into her throat. Her prospective employer possessed the knack for cutting to the heart of a matter. "I . . . used to spend my summers by the Pacific Ocean," she began. "My grandmother lived here. Not in Washington, that is, but in Oregon, along the coast. I knew that I wanted to come back someday and make my home near the Pacific." Andrea caught the ripple of emotion that had crept into her voice. *Careful,* she told herself.

"I see. You have no family in Boston then?"

She glanced down. *Family.* The word left a bitter taste in her mouth. "No," she said, meeting his eyes again. There was something in his gaze—a hint of empathy, a haunting sadness that seemed for an instant to mirror her own pain of loss. Then he looked away, and she wondered if she had only imagined that he understood. She drew in a deep breath.

"I'd welcome the opportunity to have your daughter as my

pupil," she said. She shoved aside any reservations she might have about him and tried to silence the nagging doubts that Maggie's gossip about his late wife and the number of tutors that passed through his doors raised in her head.

He cleared his throat and took another piece of paper from the folder. After inspecting it at some length, he set it aside. "Your references are nothing short of glowing," he said, offering the hint of a smile. "The position is yours, if you want it."

Her heart seemed to stumble, miss a beat. "Yes, I do. That's very good news." *I hope,* she thought.

"I would imagine you'd like to know something about my daughter and me—other than any information the agency may already have shared with you."

A certain waitress had told her more about Holt Carraday in a matter of minutes than the Manning Agency ever had. "I'd appreciate that," she said.

He gazed down at his hands. "I had Elizabeth enrolled in the public school system for two years. I thought she'd benefit by having the company of other children her age. But it didn't work out as I'd anticipated." Another long pause followed. "I'm sure you know how cruel children can be at times," he said at last.

Not just children. "The other children teased your daughter?"

He raised his head; his blue eyes flashed coldly. "It was more than simple teasing, Miss Lane."

A pang of sympathy clutched at Andrea's insides. But the expression on his face halted whatever other questions she might have wanted to ask him on the subject.

"Elizabeth was three when my wife died," he went on in a subdued voice. "She appears to remember little about her mother." He brought his hand up, ran his fingers through the tousled thickness of his hair. "I engaged the help of a psychiatrist, thinking that he could draw Elizabeth out, persuade her to express her feelings. Unfortunately, the doctor failed— though I don't fault his efforts. He told me that whatever memories Elizabeth has of her mother were likely suppressed and might never be recalled. But he also said that sometimes a certain event—perhaps a traumatic one, or perhaps one that seems insignificant—will act as a trigger and free such memories from the subconscious."

Memories. Too vivid, too painful to be recalled. "I believe I can relate to that, Mr. Carraday. My mother died when I was seven. After the funeral, I felt confused—and angry," she said quietly. "I believed that she had gone away on purpose, that she had abandoned Dad and me. It hurt me terribly, so I put away all my pictures of her and didn't take them out again for a very long time."

Another shadow seemed to pass over his face, like clouds being chased by the wind. "I'm certain that you would be the ideal tutor for Elizabeth. Will you accept my terms as drawn up by the agency?"

Andrea regained her composure. "I consider them fair. Yes, I accept your offer."

He retrieved a long piece of paper from his desk. "You'll need to sign and date this contract. Why don't you take it with you to read over, then bring it back to me tomorrow." He pushed the contract across the desk to her.

Andrea's fingers curled around the piece of paper. "Tomorrow?"

His mouth twitched in a small smile. "I see you're surprised. What I meant to say is—could you come to the house in the morning? I'd like for you to meet Elizabeth and our small staff, and I'll be available then to show you around the estate. Once you're settled in, you can inspect the educational materials we have on hand. You may decide to use them—or you may want to set up your own curriculum. The choice is yours."

Had the "educational materials" been selected by the succession of tutors before her? "That's fine," Andrea replied.

Her new employer pushed back his chair. "I'll show you to the front door."

Andrea rose. At the same instant, the clock on the mantel

chimed out the hour. The touch of a hand at Andrea's elbow caused her to look up, and she found herself staring into the glacial eyes. To have them so close to her own was disturbing enough, but to feel their owner's fingers curved around her elbow caused her discomfort of a different sort.

"It'll be night soon," Mr. Carraday said as he guided her toward the door.

They passed the painting of the *Royal Charles* and the tables with their displays of ships encased in glass. At the doorway, Andrea was drawn to a stop. "Be careful on your drive back to Seacliff. The fog rolls in at dusk."

Andrea looked up at him. "I'm always . . . careful."

"I'm glad to hear that."

In the absence of further conversation, Andrea became more aware than she wanted to be of her employer's presence at her side. The heat from his strong, lean fingers seemed to burn through the fabric of her jacket, warming her skin, and for the first time, she detected the odor of his cologne. Its heady fragrance reminded her at once of the forest and the ocean, and she thought how appropriate the scent was to a man who lived in a place called Ravenspire.

A man as compellingly handsome as Holt Carraday would attract women by the hordes. But if what the waitress had said was fact, then he was a man who kept largely to himself. Was it because he was still in torment over his wife's death— even though he had endured a loveless marriage?

A strange tapping noise drew Andrea out of her introspection, and she noticed that Mr. Carraday was slowing his pace. At the same time, his grip on her tightened. Without warning, he swung around on his heel, forcing her to turn, too.

A woman was striding toward them through the dimly lit hallway. She was tall and very thin, Andrea noted, and she wore a long, plain black dress that swung heavily around her heels as she walked. Despite the cumbersome skirt, her movements were quick and agile and sure, and she didn't appear to be in need of the cane that she thrust boldly out in front of her every time her right foot struck the floor.

When the woman's face came into view, Andrea saw that the pale skin was etched with spidery lines, and there were yellow patches on her cheeks, betraying her advanced years. Still, her features were strong, and her gray hair, swept into a loose knot at the top of her head, was generously thick.

But it wasn't the woman's clothing or her features or her hair that commanded Andrea's attention. It was her eyes. They matched Holt Carraday's perfectly, and they gazed at Andrea with such blue intensity that she turned away and sought out her employer's face instead.

His attention was riveted on the older woman. Andrea doubted he was even aware that he had withdrawn his hand from her and taken a step forward.

"Aunt Jayne," he said in a voice that made the greeting sound like a pronouncement of doom.

The woman stood, statuelike, her bony hands folded over the top of her cane, her eyes fixed on Andrea.

"Aunt Jayne."

The greater degree of authority in Holt Carraday's voice must have stirred a response in the old woman. She turned her head so that her gaze shifted the slightest bit in his direction.

"I want you to meet Andrea Lane." His tone was firm. "Miss Lane, this is my aunt, Jayne Evernham."

Under Jayne Evernham's chilling watchfulness, Andrea began to wonder if the old woman had something to do with the other tutors' sudden departures from Ravenspire. "I'm pleased to meet you, Ms. Evernham," she said, despite extremely strong feelings to the contrary.

Jayne Evernham drew herself up to her full height and sent her nephew a scathing glance. "This is the one, is it, Holt?"

Andrea's wariness increased. If Holt Carraday were a nobleman, then surely this old woman was sowing seeds of discontent in his kingdom.

"Yes. Miss Lane and I were able to come to an agreement on the terms of the contract."

"I'm sure you were," the old woman retorted as her gaze raked over Andrea again.

Those frigid eyes seemed to telegraph a warning to Andrea. *This is my home, and you have no business being here,* they flashed. Then their owner turned away.

The cane struck against the floor with even more impatience in retreating than it had on advancing. Andrea followed Jayne Evernham's progress with a certain morbid fascination until the old woman rounded the corner at the far end of the corridor. Was she headed for the tower?

Andrea regarded her employer. His jaw was clenched. "Your aunt lives at Ravenspire?" she asked with a measure of dread.

A moment passed before he responded. "Yes, Evernham is her married name. She's my mother's sister, and for almost as long as I can remember, she's lived here." He looked toward the ceiling. "I don't suppose you've changed your mind about the position, have you?"

"Why would I change my mind?"

"No reason." He clamped his mouth shut and took off at such a fast pace that Andrea had to hurry to catch up to him. They continued on in silence, and he made no move to take her arm again or pay the least attention to her until they arrived at the front door.

"Remember what I told you about the fog, Miss Lane."

Andrea tilted her head up and offered her employer a polite smile, nothing more, as she moved past him. She went out the door that he held open for her and didn't look back until she had reached the refuge of her car.

The door with its carvings of ships was shut tight. There was no sign of Mr. Carraday. Though lights burned in a few windows of Ravenspire, most of the glass panes were blank, and mist shrouded the upper part of the tower, lending it a haunted air. But it was the tower's single lighted window that commanded Andrea's gaze.

A lone figure was framed in the window. Was it Jayne Evernham? Andrea could picture the insolent old crone living in the garret, the sound of her cane echoing along the stairwell that Andrea imagined spiraled upward past the many rooms. As she watched, the light in the window flickered and went out, leaving behind only a black pane of glass.

Andrea ducked her head, hoping that whoever stood at the window hadn't noticed her curiosity. At that instant she caught a glimpse of a book that was half hidden under her coat. She pulled it out and saw that it was an Ellery Queen novel. She read aloud the title, *"There Was an Old Woman,"* and recalled the story about the wicked Cornelia Potts who brought sheer torture to every life she touched.

With a shiver, she shoved the book into her coat pocket and drove out the lane at a faster rate of speed than usual. At the end she slowed the car and glanced up at the raven that sat perched on top of the sign. The bird was regal in its bearing, but in her mind all that Andrea saw was the image of a man with glossy black hair and arctic blue eyes.

Chapter Three

The raven soared heavenward on wings the color of the midnight sky. Farther out it swept over the rolling sea, black spread against the silver of an early autumn moon.

On a rock high above the thundering waves, she stood watching the bird's lonely flight. How she had come to be on that slippery crag, she didn't know. Had she climbed its steep surface of ghostly gray stone? She looked at her hands, her shoeless feet. They were clean, without marks or abrasions. She lifted the hem of the white gown that she wore and inspected it. Filmy and fragile as the moonlight itself, the garment showed no spot of dirt as she let its soft folds slide between her fingers.

A cry rose above the sound of the waves. Through parted lips, she gave an answering cry. When she raised her eyes, she saw the raven circling ever closer. Its shiny black wings beat the air, and her heart thudded in her ears. This was no ordinary raven, and when its gaze met hers, she understood the reason for her wild response to its nearness. The eyes that stared into hers weren't black, but glacial blue. They were a man's eyes.

Andrea woke with a start, her pulse pounding in her ears. She sat up in bed and opened her eyes to darkness. Where was she? Not in her apartment, she realized. If she were home, she would be able to see the fuzzy glow from the streetlight outside her bedroom window.

The sound of waves lapping softly against stone served to clear her mind. She was near the Pacific Ocean, in room number twenty-seven of the Seacliff Inn, a continent away from her apartment in Boston.

"Ravenspire." The word echoed in the darkness, and she remembered the bizarre dream she'd just had about a raven—a raven that possessed Holt Carraday's eyes.

Andrea groped for her glasses on the bedside table. She found them, put them on. Then she felt her way across the small room to the window. Pulling back a corner of the heavy drape, she looked out on a parking lot that was wet with rain. The sound she'd believed was the ocean was the splash of raindrops on the pavement. Water streaked the window and dripped down from the eaves of the roof.

"Let's go for a walk in the rain, Andy." Nanna's gentle voice would nudge Andrea away from the window in her grandmother's cozy living room. Andrea would giggle and squirm as Nanna bundled her in her yellow slicker. Then off the two of them would go—without their umbrellas. *"Why be out in the rain,"* Nanna would say, *"if you can't feel it on your face and taste it on your tongue?"* And Andrea would look up into the night sky and stick out her tongue to catch the cool drops.

Did Holt Carraday take Elizabeth for walks in the rain? Did they laugh together and catch raindrops on their tongues?

Suddenly, Andrea wished that her father had taken her out in the rain, like Nanna. She groaned softly in the silence of the room. Why was she thinking of him, wishing after all these years for something that was impossible? Weren't her memories of Nanna enough? *No,* that familiar voice inside her said. *Memories are never enough.*

"Child, you can do whatever you set your mind to. The only one in the world who can keep you from making your dreams come true is yourself." Nanna had told Andrea that during a walk in the rain. It was the summer before Nanna died.

Andrea had plans—and dreams. She would teach at the academy, save her money, get married, and open a private tutoring service. And one day she would have children of her own. For a while it seemed as if her dreams would come true. Until that bitterly cold and snowy December night when the edge of a cold steel blade at her cheek shattered her hopes and destroyed her innocence.

Nanna had told Andrea something else that last summer they were together. *"You're a survivor, Andy,"* she'd said. Andrea had been too young at the time to understand the wisdom of her grandmother's words. But she understood them now.

"You were right, Nanna. I am a survivor," she whispered, letting the curtain fall back, sealing out the view of the night and the rain.

Andrea found her way to the bathroom and switched on the light. Under its harsh fluorescent glare, she took a glass from its wrapper and poured herself a drink of water, avoiding the reflection of herself in the mirror. When she set the glass down, she caught a glimpse of her image. Her gaze was arrested by what she saw. Her hair fell over her forehead in a jumbled mass of curls and waves. The scar seemed to stand out in garish contrast to the paleness of her skin. Or was it her imagination? What had Holt Carraday seen when he'd looked at her face? Maybe he'd been relieved, had decided she would prove to be no temptation to him. Maybe he'd even imagined that she would be content to live at Ravenspire and tutor his daughter for as long as he wanted her there.

Andrea turned away from the mirror. The truth was it didn't matter what his reasons were for hiring her. The fact that she found herself attracted to him was something she'd have to get used to. That should be easy enough, since he was as remote as he was handsome.

Besides, shouldn't she have learned her lesson with men by now? Alan had been an excellent teacher. There were no fairy-tale romances, no gallant knights on white horses who rode up to rescue the princess in distress. There were only knaves who stole a princess's heart and crushed it beneath their feet. And the moral of the story was that the princess learned to take care of herself.

Andrea flipped off the bathroom light and returned to bed, secure in the knowledge that any interest Mr. Carraday might express toward her was certain to be of a strictly professional nature. Still, when she closed her eyes, she prayed that if she ever dreamed again of a raven with glacial blue eyes, she would have no memory of it when she wakened.

"Holt Carraday hired you, didn't he?"

Andrea glanced up at Maggie from the booth where she was ready to order her breakfast. "Yes, he did."

Maggie frowned. "What'd you think of him?"

Andrea looked out the window. Where rain had glazed the parking lot hours ago, now the sun shone, drawing steam from the pavement. "Mr. Carraday struck me as rather... formal." *No,* she almost added, *he's as cold as the Pacific on a winter's day.*

"I wouldn't wonder at that, dear. Word is that he was sent off to boarding school quite young—to England, I understand. No doubt he picked up all those British ways and manners. It's where he met his wife, too, they say. But I would've thought you'd be more taken with him."

Andrea hid a smile. Maggie reminded her more and more of a mother hen—a nosy one, to be sure.

"Did Ravenspire strike you as formal, too?"

The waitress's quiet question surprised Andrea. How to describe Carraday's castle—or the forbidding old woman who held court there? Maybe Maggie wasn't even aware of Jayne Evernham's existence.

Just then a man's voice shouted for the waitress. It wasn't the cook this time, but a customer, though the sharp command had the same effect on Maggie. She let out a gasp. "Sorry, dear," she said, "I've got to run." She started off, then stopped when Andrea called her back.

"Before you go, Maggie, could I put in my order?"

The waitress's cheeks turned rosy. "Of course, dear." She scribbled notes on her pad as Andrea gave her selection of French toast and a cup of hot tea. "I'll come back as soon as I can," the waitress promised, "and we'll talk some more."

But Maggie was kept busy by the rush of customers that crowded into the café. It wasn't until she bustled by with Andrea's food that she managed to get in a final word. Darting a look over her shoulder—perhaps for the dreaded Charlie—she bent close to Andrea. "I see you're without your glasses this morning. You know, your eyes are very beautiful—and so is your hair. You're an attractive young woman at that, dear."

Before Andrea could make a reply, Maggie went on in a confidential tone, "I do pray that you'll stay on your toes and keep yourself safe in that frightening old mansion. And you will come in and let me know how you're getting along, won't you?"

Andrea's mouth fell open. *"Your eyes are very beautiful. So is your hair. Stay on your toes . . . keep yourself safe."* Maggie's words echoed in her ears. "I'll stop in," she said at last. But the waitress had already moved on to take an order at the next booth, and Andrea's promise was lost in the din of conversation that swirled around her.

The drive to Ravenspire proved uneventful, and in the fresh light of morning, even the sight of Holt Carraday's castle failed to dampen Andrea's sudden sense of optimism. *Everything will work out for the best,* she thought. *I've made the right decision.* She found herself looking forward to meeting Elizabeth Carraday.

The same fair-haired woman as before welcomed Andrea at the front door of Ravenspire. "My name's Laura," the woman said as Andrea stepped into the foyer. "I'm Mr. Carraday's housekeeper, though you've probably figured that out." She smiled, and her face looked almost pretty.

Andrea returned the housekeeper's smile. Laura impressed her as genuinely nice. She thought, too, that the foyer looked more inviting than it had the day before. Sunshine streamed through the long windows flanking the door, lending the room a cheerful glow. The light illumined one of the paintings on the wall, and Andrea noticed that in the portrait, the somber gray stones of the mansion were enhanced with generous splashes of lavender and rose, transforming the home into a true castle. All that was missing was the damsel in distress at one of the tower windows and the knight in shining armor charging to her rescue. *There are no brave knights,* she reminded herself.

"Mr. Carraday's mother, Grace, painted that view of Ravenspire," Laura commented.

"Is that so? She must have been very talented. It's a lovely rendering."

"The house looks just like that at sunset."

Andrea doubted that Ravenspire had ever looked that magical, though she didn't question the housekeeper's sincerity. "Have you worked at Ravenspire a long time, Laura?"

"It'll be twelve years next month for my husband, John, and me."

"Your husband's employed here too?"

"He's the chief groundskeeper." Laura smiled again. "I'm sure Mr. Carraday plans on introducing you to him this morning, along with Carl."

"Carl?"

"He's in charge of the stables." Laura clasped her hands over her apron. "We're a small staff here at Ravenspire, just four full-time employees, including the cook, Sybil. Since most of the rooms are no longer in use, and with Mr. Carraday rarely entertaining guests since his . . . since he became a widower, the four of us manage pretty well."

Andrea thought of the closed doors they'd passed the day before, and she pictured the rooms behind them as dark, their furnishings faded and covered in dust sheets. Did Laura intend to lead her down the same hallway to the study with its paintings and models of ships in glass bottles?

"Come with me," Laura said, and she started off in the opposite direction, taking the corridor that formed the west wing of Ravenspire—the one that led to the tower. "I'll tell

John to bring in your luggage, Miss Lane," she said over her shoulder.

Luggage? Did that mean she was expected to move in that very morning? "I don't have any with me. That is, I have one suitcase—at the motel." Along with two more nights' deposit on her room, she could have added.

Laura's steps slowed. "You have just one?"

"I'm afraid I hadn't counted on moving in quite so soon." Not that she'd need a great deal of time to make the transition from Boston to Ravenspire. She'd already made arrangements to sublet her apartment, pending the outcome of her interview, and she'd severed most of her ties to the city—at least in her mind—the minute she'd boarded the plane for the West Coast.

Laura gave a soft laugh. It seemed the housekeeper's every movement reflected a gentle, passive nature. "I understand, but as you get better acquainted with Mr. Carraday, you'll learn that he likes to take immediate action once he's made up his mind on a matter that he considers important to him."

"I appreciate knowing that."

The housekeeper smiled, but said no more until she came to a set of double doors with carved ivory handles.

"Mr. Carraday asked that I bring you to the Grand Hall." She pulled on the handles and the doors creaked open.

"Grand" hardly did justice to the hall that opened up before Andrea. The sheer size of the room was breathtaking—and impossible to take in with a sweeping glance. Its length could easily encompass a half dozen average living rooms, and along its walls stood great archways supported by columns of white marble that soared upward from the blue tiled floor to the domed ceiling.

A blue-and-white theme predominated throughout the Grand Hall. The blue was repeated in a hundred varying shades in the fabrics of the ancient-looking sofas and love seats and chairs that were arranged in formal groupings, and in more subtle ways in the Ming jars and Wedgwood vases and lamps that accented the occasional tables. A huge faded tapestry of a blue unicorn hung on one wall, but there were no paintings of ships nor miniatures encased in glass anywhere in sight.

Had the Carradays hosted their parties in the Grand Hall? Andrea could envision the splendor, the men and women dressed to the nines, holding glasses of wine or flutes of champagne in their hands. There might be a lavish buffet dinner and, of course, afterward an orchestra and dancing. She could almost hear the sweet strains of the orchestra as it played beneath one of those majestic arches, smell the heady fragrance of the women's perfume, feel the touch of a man's hand on her shoulder as he bent to ask her to dance. And, for a moment, Andrea forgot why she was there.

The sight of her new employer rising from a chair at the far end of the Grand Hall reminded her. He was silhouetted by a pair of glass doors, the only doors or windows in the room, Andrea realized. He motioned to her with his hand. Then he did a puzzling thing. He pulled shut the drapes over the doors before he walked in her direction.

Today he wore a plain white polo shirt and faded jeans that were tucked into black leather boots. The breath caught in Andrea's throat as he strode toward her. Holt Carraday's presence suddenly filled the Grand Hall, filled Andrea's mind as well, and made her think unsettling thoughts about knights and castles and maidens dancing the night away in their lovers' arms.

"Good morning." He stopped in front of her.

"Good morning, Mr. Carraday." Locked in a stare with him, she wondered whimsically if, out of all the shades of blue in the Grand Hall, any of them could equal the blue of his eyes.

"Your glasses. Did something happen to them?"

"Nothing happened to them, but I'm used to wearing contacts." The way he was staring at her—did he find something to criticize in the magenta skirt and ivory silk blouse that she wore? Had he just noticed the scar? She'd worn her hair in the same conservative style as the day before, and she'd taken care in applying her makeup.

He lifted one brow. "Contacts. Of course." Moving away from her, he said, "Elizabeth will be joining us in a few minutes, but there's something else I'd like to show you first."

Andrea watched curiously as he walked to the other end of the room and stopped near the double doors that led to the corridor.

"Don't be frightened," he called to her. "I'm going to turn out the lights."

Before Andrea could react, the Grand Hall was plunged into complete darkness. Despite his warning, the unfamiliarity of her surroundings caused Andrea to become disoriented and, for a second, she panicked.

Then her temper flared. What strange game was her new employer playing with her, anyway? Was he bent on testing the mettle of her courage? If so, she would soon show him that she could keep her cool. She could also tear up the contract, which she had stashed in her purse in the car, and tell him that he could start looking for another tutor for his daughter.

"Now look up at the ceiling, Miss Lane."

Irked by the authoritative tone of his voice, Andrea nonetheless followed his orders. A sense of awe, of wonder, replaced the anger as she stared wide-eyed at the ceiling of the Grand Hall. It was no longer a plain ceiling but one that had been magically transformed into a night sky, complete with twinkling stars and a shimmering slice of a silver moon.

"If you'd glance a little to your left, you'll see a cluster of stars. Do you recognize them?"

Her eyes picked out the stars. Should she know them? "I see the stars, but I'm not sure . . ."

"They're Orion."

The figure came into clear focus. "Yes, the hunter with his bow."

"Watch carefully."

She watched, and the stars began to move. Or were her eyes playing tricks on her? They were definitely not playing tricks, she realized when Holt Carraday said to her, "Orion is making his journey across the winter sky."

Andrea knew that the show on the ceiling of the Grand Hall was as real as the presence of the man who had come to stand beside her.

"It's . . . incredible," she said. "I've never seen anything like it before." She sensed he moved in some direction. His throaty chuckle told Andrea that he had drawn closer to her. It seemed she could feel the heat from his body warming her skin, and she thought that if she were to move an inch, their hands would soon touch, his fingertips would brush hers in passing. The notion caused her to stand very still.

"For as long as I can recall, Miss Lane," he said at last, "my mother wished for a piece of the sky to look up at whenever she pleased."

"This was your mother's idea?" Andrea turned her face toward him. She could just make out his tall, shadowy form in the faint glow from the make-believe stars and moon.

"Grace Carraday was an amazing woman. Intelligent. And tenacious. She came up with a plan, a sketch, which she persuaded me to show to a friend of mine who also happened to be an architectural engineer. He studied the plan, said that it was feasible. So a piece of the sky was installed at Ravenspire."

"That must have made your mother very happy . . . to watch her dream come true." *I know I would be happy.*

"It would have made her happy, I believe, if she'd lived long enough."

"She never got to see all of this?"

"No."

"But you went on with the project."

"Anything worthwhile should be brought to its completion, don't you think?"

"Yes," she said softly, adding, "Your daughter must enjoy watching the show."

"Elizabeth hasn't come into the Grand Hall since shortly after her mother's death." A note of frustration threaded through his voice. "One evening after dinner, Laura found her here. Elizabeth was crying. From then on, she refused to set foot in the room."

"I'm sorry."

"I'm hopeful that as she gets to know you, Miss Lane, she'll be able to conquer some of her fears."

What moved him to place such confidence in her? Before Andrea could reply, he said, "It's over," and when she gazed at the ceiling, she saw that Orion had finished his journey across the make-believe sky.

"Now," he said, "it's time for—"

A loud knock interrupted him. There was the sound of a door being opened, then a shaft of light spread across the floor of the Hall.

"Mr. Carraday?"

"Come in, Laura," he said, "and put the lamps on."

The Grand Hall suddenly glowed with light. Laura was visible, hovering by the door.

"Where's Elizabeth?"

The housekeeper came forward. "I'm sorry, Mr. Carraday, but she wasn't in her room."

He frowned. "I specifically told Elizabeth to stay there until you came for her."

"I know, sir." Laura glanced uncertainly from her employer to Andrea. "I called John to ask if he'd seen her."

"And?" Holt prompted.

"He had, but it was a while ago, I'm afraid. He said she was headed for the stable barn at the time."

"All right." Holt sighed. "I'll find her, Laura. Thank you."

Andrea looked at her employer, and the sense of wonder she'd known moments before vanished. What kind of relationship did father and daughter have? A distant one, she suspected. Something Maggie had said about Victoria

Carraday came back to haunt her. *"They say the child's the picture of her."*

"Miss Lane."

Andrea blinked. "Yes, Mr. Carraday?"

He raked a hand impatiently through his hair. "I'd like for you to . . ." His mouth snapped shut, and he looked at her. Then his expression subtly shifted, and there was a slight softening in the set of his jaw. "Please come with me. You might as well see some of the grounds while we're hunting for Elizabeth."

Torn between feelings of relief and uneasiness, Andrea merely nodded. If he'd asked her to wait for him inside the mansion, there was the chance she might run into Jayne Evernham, a particularly unpleasant notion. But the idea of witnessing a confrontation between father and daughter held little appeal, either. *Nothing like being caught between a rock and a hard place,* she told herself.

Together, they passed the archways and marble pillars. Just before they stepped into the corridor, he turned off the lamps.

Andrea stopped on the threshold of the Grand Hall, unable to resist glancing back. Her gaze drifted to the domed ceiling and the small piece of sky that was embedded there. But she saw only blackness. When Mr. Carraday called her name, she turned to join him in the corridor.

They walked, without speaking, down the hallway toward a door that Andrea deduced led up to the tower. Was she going to have to face Jayne Evernham after all? But when they came to the end, there was no sign of the old woman with her cane, only more closed doors, one to the left, the other straight ahead.

Mr. Carraday opened the door that was in front of them and motioned for Andrea to go through. She was released from the cryptlike mansion into a benevolent world of sunshine and blue sky. But she couldn't help sliding a glance at the tower and wondering if Jayne Evernham was watching from some lofty angle inside.

"It's called the Raven's Roost, Miss Lane."

Andrea drew in a swift, sharp breath as she observed Holt Carraday's face lit by the afternoon sun. His eyes were sapphires, shining down at her; fine lines etched the corners of each eye—proof to Andrea that he had once been a man who smiled easily. But the blue depths were guarded now, the corners of his mouth turned down as if he had forgotten how to laugh.

"My aunt lives in the Roost," he said, lifting his gaze to the tower. He shielded his eyes with the back of his hand.

So the tower was the old woman's lair, just as Andrea had thought. "It looks . . . spacious," she said. The topmost window of the Raven's Roost stood open; dark, voluminous curtains flapped in the wind that blew from the west. "Your aunt strikes me as being a very private person, Mr. Carraday."

"She's a recluse."

There was no prelude to the chilly blast of air that came howling around the corner of the tower. The cold crept through Andrea, and she thought how unpredictable the weather could be that time of year. In summer, the wind's frigidness was usually tempered by the warmth of the sun, though Nanna would still warn lovingly, *"Button that sweater up tight now, Andy, so you don't catch a chill."*

"You're smiling, Miss Lane." He regarded her with interest.

"The wind blowing like that made me think of something my grandmother used to tell me."

His eyebrows arched, though he made no reply nor gave any indication that he'd been affected by the unfavorable shift in the weather. But Andrea shivered as she threw a last glance at the tower. There was movement of some sort at the window. Andrea tensed until she caught a glimpse of blondish hair. *Laura must be there, cleaning the old woman's rooms,* she thought. At least it wasn't Jayne spying on her nephew and the new tutor.

Mr. Carraday led her down a flagstone path that wound between two rows of high evergreen hedges. Finally, they emerged near a stone building with a gabled roof.

A man came charging around the corner of the building, his head bowed against the wind.

"Carl."

The man's head popped up. "Mr. Carraday."

"This is Miss Lane, our new tutor. Miss Lane, Carl Stubin. Carl's in charge of our small stable of horses."

Dressed in tan riding breeches and a black sweater and matching cap, the short, wiry man looked like an aging jockey. "Glad to meet you," he said, but his expression told her otherwise.

Undeterred, Andrea extended her hand to him. "Nice to meet you, Carl." His hand, cool and calloused, took hers in a tight, almost painful grip.

"Have you seen my daughter?" Holt asked.

Carl took off his cap, put it back on again. "She's in the barn, sir. Grooming Patches."

Everything about Carl—the jerky movement of his arm, the constant shifting of his feet, the momentary twitch in his cheek—betrayed an air of nervousness. Was his discomfort due to fear that he was setting Elizabeth up for possible punishment? Following Holt Carraday into the barn, Andrea offered Carl a tentative smile. His frown and the narrowing of his eyes seemed to indicate that, like Jayne Evernham, he had marked her with his disapproval.

It took a moment for Andrea to adjust to the dim interior. Gradually, she could make out the shapes of the box stalls and the horses that occupied three of them. A dappled mare observed Andrea placidly from the first stall. From the next, a huge roan ignored her as he munched on his hay.

"That's Rusty, Carl's gelding," Holt explained with a gesture in the roan's direction.

The third stall held an impressive white stallion. "Easy, Admiral." Holt stopped to give the horse a pat, then moved on. "Elizabeth?" he called out.

Admiral nickered once, twice. Finally, a small figure materialized from behind the last stall. A halo of blond curls stood out against the dark walls, but the child's face was hidden from view.

"There you are."

Elizabeth stood still, not responding to her father.

"Miss Lane."

The touch of a hand on her arm caused Andrea to give a start. Her gaze shifted from daughter to father.

"I think it would be best if you waited outside."

What had she done, taking for granted that he welcomed her presence inside the stable? "Yes, of course," she said, turning quickly away.

Andrea closed the door behind her and leaned against the rough stone wall. Her head throbbed with the beginnings of a headache. She looked around for Carl but saw no sign of him. It appeared he'd gone elsewhere. With a sigh, she massaged her temples and steeled herself for the moment when Holt and his daughter emerged from the barn.

Chapter Four

"Miss Lane."

Andrea's eyes flew open. She hadn't heard his approach, but when she turned she saw her employer standing next to her. He motioned for her to come with him. She was too conscious of his attentiveness, the brief, firm touch of his fingers at her elbow, guiding her as they went into the barn.

He took the lead ahead of her down the wide center aisle. "Go on in," he said when they approached the last stall.

Andrea found herself facing the rump of a small brown-and-white pony. Its tail swished past her face, narrowly missing her cheek.

"Don't be scared. Patches won't hurt you."

The timid assurance came from the shadowy recess at the other end of the stall.

Squinting, Andrea made out the blond hair, then the slight figure of Elizabeth Carraday. The child was standing by the pony's left front quarter, a currying brush in her hand. "I'm not afraid of Patches." Andrea moved cautiously toward the girl. "He just caught me by surprise, that's all."

"She," a masculine voice said.

"What..." Andrea looked over her shoulder; Mr. Carraday was right behind her.

"Patches is a *she*."

"Oh... yes." Andrea turned slightly and found that she was sandwiched between Patches and her employer. For a moment she was distracted by Holt's nearness in the confines of the stall. Though his manner was as cold as the sea on a starless night, his blue gaze drew Andrea as a ship is drawn

39

to a beacon in the midst of the cruel sea. And she reacted in the same manner as she had when he'd stood beside her in the Grand Hall with the lamps turned off and only the imitation stars for light. She stood perfectly still.

"I think Patches has had enough brushing for today," he spoke quietly to his daughter. His breath warmed Andrea's cheek, further distracting her. He reached around her and took hold of Elizabeth's arm. "Elizabeth, I want you to meet your new teacher." He coaxed her in Andrea's direction. "This is Miss Lane."

As soon as Elizabeth turned fully, Andrea could see that she was very delicate and beautiful in appearance, with large, luminous eyes that peered curiously up at the new tutor and hair that was almost more silver in tone than blond. For a moment, Andrea was surprised by how little Elizabeth resembled her father. Their noses were similar, but that was about all.

But if the child was the image of her mother, as Maggie had said, then Andrea felt as if she'd been given a glimpse of Victoria Carraday's beauty. Kneeling down so that she was eye level with the girl, she said, "I'm very happy to meet you, Elizabeth."

A look of uncertainty passed over the child's face, and her cupid's-bow mouth opened slightly. But she didn't speak until her father gave her a visible nudge. "Hello," she said in a small, timid voice.

No one made a move until finally Holt cleared his throat. "Please put the brush away, Elizabeth. It's time we went back to the house. Sybil will have lunch ready, and you'll need to clean up before you eat."

The little girl looked at the brush in her hand, then at Andrea. "Do you like horses?" she asked.

The expression of shy interest on Elizabeth's face made Andrea smile. "I like horses a lot, but ponies in particular." She gently stroked Patches and spoke softly to her for a moment.

Holt led the way from the stall. "Miss Lane used to give

riding lessons," he said to his daughter. "Maybe you can show her some of the trails that you and Patches like to explore."

Elizabeth turned again to Andrea. "Is Shadow going to be your horse?" She walked over to the stall that held the dappled mare.

Andrea shot a questioning glance at her employer.

"It's up to you, Miss Lane," he said. "Would you like to ride Shadow?"

"If it's all right with you, Mr. Carraday."

"It's all right with me." His mouth tilted in the suggestion of a smile.

When Elizabeth stepped into the stall, the mare tossed its head and whinnied. "Shadow was Auntie Jayne's horse," the girl declared.

Andrea stared warily at the animal. "Shadow is Mrs. Evernham's horse?"

"Was," corrected Holt. "Mrs. Evernham hasn't ridden the mare in years."

"But Auntie Jayne comes to the barn sometimes to groom Shadow," Elizabeth spoke up.

Andrea observed as Elizabeth stroked the mare. The girl's hand looked tiny against the wide, spotted flank. "I think it might be better if I had another horse to ride, instead."

"Why?" Holt asked with a hint of impatience. "Is there something wrong with the mare?"

Like its former mistress, the animal seemed to glare at Andrea. "No. I'm sure that Shadow and I will get along just fine."

"The matter's settled then," Holt said. He turned and led the way out of the barn.

Elizabeth skipped along in front of her father on the path. After she'd gone a few yards, she came to a stop and gazed toward Andrea. In full daylight, the pixielike face displayed a vulnerable quality that reminded Andrea of a delicate wildflower growing in oppressive shade when what it craves most is the warmth of the sun.

Andrea's protective instincts rallied, and she had the crazy impulse to scoop the girl up in her arms and assure her that everything would be all right. Instead, she smiled and waved to Elizabeth.

The girl sprinted on ahead while her father strolled in silence beside Andrea. They passed several artfully arranged beds of creeping ivy and fall flowers that were past their prime.

"You should have seen the marigolds and mums when they were in full bloom." Holt made a gesture toward the flower beds. "It was my wife's idea. She planted the beds some years ago. Their colors in autumn," he said quietly, "remind me of the sun when it sets over the water."

Andrea stared at the drooping heads of the flowers. Victoria had planted them, and now whenever Holt passed by the beds, he must remember his wife. Looking up, Andrea met eyes as enigmatic as the ocean. For an instant she thought she saw regret in them. And guilt. Would he endure a loveless marriage again—if, indeed, that was what it had been—to have Victoria there, alive, fussing over the marigolds and mums that made him think of a sunset?

Like an open window that is quickly closed, Holt lowered his eyes from Andrea and moved past her and the sleeping beds of flowers.

Take care, Andrea told herself. Who was she to draw conclusions about a man she barely knew—based solely on the gossip of a waitress at the local café? She recalled something her grandmother had once said when Andrea had found a fatally wounded sparrow and cried because she couldn't save it. *"If you had your way, Andy, you'd protect every living thing around you. You want to fix every hurt. But there're some hurts that can't be healed, no matter how hard we try."*

Who had learned the truth of Nanna's words better than her own granddaughter? *Maybe Holt Carraday has hurts, too, that can't be healed,* she thought. *Or maybe I'm only imagining it.*

They walked on without talking. A short distance ahead,

they approached a man dressed in baggy coveralls. He was perched on a ladder that was propped against a tree. He held a pair of pruning shears in his hands.

"John. I'd like for you to meet Miss Lane, our new tutor." Holt motioned to the tall, sandy-haired man.

John stepped down from the ladder and set the pruning shears aside. "Pleased to meet you," he said, extending his hand to Andrea.

She immediately warmed to the man whose pleasant manner mirrored his wife's. "Nice to meet you, too, John."

With a smile and a nod of the head, John picked up the shears and mounted the ladder again.

"Laura told me that she and John have worked at Ravenspire for twelve years."

"That's right." Holt shoved his hands in his pockets and gazed down at the path. "I highly value their loyalty," he said after a long pause.

Though she didn't respond, the implication wasn't lost on Andrea. Would she be loyal, too, like John and Laura? Or would she give him her notice before the ink had a chance to dry on her contract? Was that what the other tutors had done? Or had he dismissed them, as Maggie had conjectured?

When they neared the house, Holt called to his daughter, "Don't forget to wash up." Turning to Andrea, he said, "Come with me," and then he took another path that veered off from the first.

A pitch-roofed, one-story stone building loomed in front of them. "The garage," Holt announced, leading Andrea around the building to the other side.

The garage door was standing open. Housed in the garage were a late-model silver Lexus and a red Toyota sedan with a dented right fender and a flat tire.

"Though the Toyota isn't much to look at, John generally keeps it in running order." Holt opened the driver's side door and tinkered with a knob on the dashboard. "Leasing a car can be very expensive," he said, "and unless you're planning to drive a car out from Boston, you're welcome to use this one."

He stepped back, and Andrea peered into the interior of the Toyota. The upholstery was a bit shabby but in otherwise good repair. Having the car at her disposal would be nice, since she had no intention of driving her own aging Civic across the country. She walked around the Toyota a couple of times, then stopped and gazed quizzically at the flat tire.

Holt came forward, his face set in a wry expression. "Don't worry. John will make sure the car is roadworthy by the time you're back."

Andrea smiled. "Then I'll take you up on your offer, Mr. Carraday."

He went to the other side of the garage and returned in a few long strides. "The keys. In case I'm gone when you return." He dropped them into her hand. "How long will you need to square things away in Boston?"

His question took a moment to register. Her mind was working on the other thing he'd said. *"The keys. In case I'm gone when you return."*

"Miss Lane?"

"Yes. . . ."

"Is a week enough? Or will you need two?"

"No, a week is fine," she said.

He took her back by way of yet another path that converged with the first near the house. Andrea darted a glance at the tower as she went by, but its windows gave away nothing, and she looked straight ahead as she went through the door of the mansion.

With the daylight shut out, the darkness of Ravenspire seemed to press in on Andrea again. When she passed the ivory-handled doors, she pictured the star show on the ceiling and the thousand shades of blue reflected in the furnishings of the Grand Hall. She remembered, too, Holt's revelation that Laura had found his daughter crying in the Grand Hall and that Elizabeth hadn't set foot in the place since. *Why?* Andrea wanted to ask. Had the girl wandered there, distraught over the loss of her mother? Or had something happened in the Grand Hall that frightened her and made her fearful of ever entering the room again?

"You will eat lunch with us?" Holt asked.

"Yes, of course."

They came to the foyer. "The bedrooms are on the second floor," Holt said, indicating a carpeted stairwell.

Andrea peered up. The stairs looked as dark and uninviting as the rest of Ravenspire.

"Sybil's quarters are off the kitchen," Holt went on, "and Carl has a couple of rooms at the rear of the barn. John and Laura live in a coach house on the grounds."

They proceeded down the other corridor to a door near the end. Holt pushed open the door, revealing a half bath. "In case you'd like to freshen up."

Andrea stepped inside and shut the door behind her. When she finished washing her hands in the sink, she found Holt waiting for her across the corridor. He stood leaning against the wall, one leg crossed over the other. He looked relaxed, but there was a hesitancy in his movements as he came toward her, a wariness that made her think of the first distant flash of lightning before an advancing storm.

Andrea's blood quickened. She knew all about wariness. Her hand automatically came up to touch the scar, and she had to deliberately lower her arm to her side. It seemed the last few months the scar had become more and more a reminder of Alan's unreasonable expectations of her and of how hopes and dreams could be shattered in an instant of time.

Perhaps you and I are not so very different, she thought as she faced Holt. *We're both trying to hide our scars.*

Holt turned away and opened another door. "The dining room," he said, ushering her inside.

The room Andrea entered was immense and dreary. The lower portion of each wall was paneled in dark wood, the upper portion covered with dull flocked wallpaper.

A mammoth rectangular table graced with a white linen cloth and surrounded by eight carved wooden chairs dominated the middle of the room, while a massive sideboard held court along one wall. Paintings of ships decorated the opposite wall; next to the largest painting was a closed door that led who knew where. An unlit brass chandelier hung above the table, while sunlight filtered wanly into the room from a row of four narrow leaded windows.

Three settings of silverware, plates, and water goblets already filled with water and ice were arranged at the end of the table nearest the windows. Two candelabras stood in the center of the table.

"Why don't you sit here, Miss Lane."

He assisted her with her chair, then went around the table to sit opposite her.

Soon after, Elizabeth appeared and climbed into the chair beside her father's. The girl's silvery blond hair gleamed in the light from the windows.

An uneasy silence fell over the room, broken when Mr. Carraday said, "I think we're having one of your favorites, Elizabeth—lamb stew."

Andrea had never eaten lamb, but she had about as much enthusiasm to try it as she'd had to eat the veal cutlet at The Timbers Café. Discreetly, she observed Elizabeth. The child sat at attention in her chair, her hands under the table, with all the timidity of a tiny mouse.

Shortly, Laura came gliding through the door nearest the painting. She carried a large white tureen in her hands, which she set on the table in front of Mr. Carraday. Behind her followed a short, stocky woman with bleached blond hair and coarse features.

"Sybil, let me introduce you to Miss Lane."

The woman regarded Andrea with pale gray eyes. "H'lo, Miss Lane," she said in a low, gruff voice. Her hands were clenched together over her white apron, and huge silver earrings dangled from her ears, flashing as they caught the light.

"I'm pleased to meet you," Andrea said, all the while wondering how Ravenspire had managed to attract such a disparate group of employees to work within its grim walls.

An appetizing smell wafted through the air when Sybil lifted the lid on the tureen. The cook proceeded to ladle portions of stew onto the plates. A bit of gravy sloshed onto the tablecloth as she served Andrea's portion. She threw a glance at Andrea but didn't offer an apology.

"I'll bring the rolls in," said Laura, and the two women left the room.

Andrea took her cue from her employer. He and his daughter had their heads bent over their plates in identical poses as they began to eat their lunch. Andrea speared a carrot slice with her fork. The bite went down easily enough, and she took another before glancing up again. Holt's eyes connected with hers, and they stared at each other for a moment. Then he returned his attention to his plate.

After what seemed an eternity Laura appeared with the rolls. "Tell Sybil that the stew is excellent," Holt said. "One more thing, Laura," he added as the housekeeper started off. "After lunch, I'd like for you to show Miss Lane her rooms."

Laura nodded and smiled in Andrea's direction. "It'll be my pleasure," she said.

Was every meal like this? Andrea wondered after Laura had left. A strained affair conducted in an atmosphere more reminiscent of a morgue than a dining room? It could be worse, she told herself. Jayne Evernham could be seated at the table, too.

"Dad, may I be excused?"

The thin, childish voice sounded a plaintive note, drawing Andrea's gaze across the table.

"You haven't eaten your lunch," Holt Carraday pointed out to his daughter.

"I'm full," she whispered, though her portion of stew looked as if it hadn't been touched.

"All right, Elizabeth, you're excused. But you know the rules. There won't be anything except your afternoon snack of milk and cookies to tide you over until dinner tonight."

"Yes, Dad." The girl pushed her chair back and fled the room without so much as a backward glance.

Holt sighed. "I apologize for my daughter's rudeness, Miss Lane."

"No apology is necessary. Elizabeth wasn't rude. I'm sure her actions were due to her . . . reticence. I was shy, too, when I was her age."

He seemed to study her. "I wonder if you're still shy."

"Not shy, Mr. Carraday." She smiled, recalling her reply when he warned her about the fog. "I'm just careful. Remember?"

"That's right. Careful." His mouth crooked slightly before he went back to eating.

They finished their meal without further conversation. After a dessert of fresh fruit and cheese was served, Laura returned, and Holt gave Andrea instructions to come to his study with her contract when she was done inspecting her rooms.

Laura led the way up the stairwell. The second floor corridor was narrow with a flat ceiling and the usual sparse lighting and shadowy corners.

"Mr. Carraday's rooms," Laura announced with a slight sweep of her hand as they passed the first door on the right.

Are they the rooms he used to share with his wife? Andrea questioned as she glanced at the tightly closed door. *Or did he move to different quarters after her death?*

Laura's steps slowed as they neared a door that stood ajar.

An instrumental arrangement of a familiar-sounding children's tune that Andrea couldn't quite identify wafted out from the room.

"It's been difficult for her," Laura said, her mild voice sounding even more hushed than usual. "With her father being gone so much, and with no other children for company. I do think . . ." Laura sighed. "What I mean to say, Miss Lane, is . . ."

The simple tune faded away. There was a brief pause, then another one began. This time the notes were accompanied by a child's high-pitched singing. Andrea raised her eyes to meet Laura's. "Please, just call me Andrea."

"Sure . . . Andrea." The housekeeper offered another of

her gentle smiles. "I didn't mean to give the impression that Mr. Carraday neglects his daughter." She resumed walking. "It's just that, since Mrs. Carraday's... death, John and I have made an effort to help out a bit more, include Elizabeth in a few of our activities. Occasionally, we take her to town with us, to the movies. Things like that."

"What about Mr. Carraday's aunt... Jayne Evernham?" Andrea had a hard time getting the name out.

Laura's features tightened visibly. "Mrs. Evernham has always been very attentive to Elizabeth, naturally." The housekeeper paused, then went on in a manner that gave the impression she'd rather not comment on the subject. "She hasn't been quite the same since Victoria Carraday died. Mrs. Evernham prefers to stay mostly to herself and often comes down only for dinner."

"I see." The idea that she would have to bear the old woman's company—and her scrutiny—for one meal a day was enough to kill Andrea's appetite for even the best of Sybil's cooking. But the housekeeper's observations bore out Holt's remark that his aunt was a recluse.

"In my opinion, Andrea," the housekeeper said, "your presence at Ravenspire is exactly what Elizabeth needs. Oh, here we are," she added as they neared the end of the corridor.

In front of them was a table that held the clay bust of a man's head. The housekeeper reached out and brushed some speck of dust or dirt from the statue. Then she opened the last door on the left of the hallway. "These are your rooms," she announced.

The bedroom, Andrea noticed immediately, was decidedly Victorian in its decor, and cozy. The walls were papered in a delicate white-and-mauve floral motif. An elaborately carved walnut bed stood against the far wall. Its white canopy and numerous pillows and bolsters sent Andrea a silent invitation to come curl up under the downy teal comforter and be lulled into a sleep of peaceful dreams.

Beside the bed was a matching walnut night table topped

with a rose-hued antique glass lamp. A cedar chest stood at the base of the bed, and a mahogany bureau of serpentine design reminiscent of the one Nanna had owned was tucked in a corner.

Laura led Andrea through a wide archway into a small sitting room. At one end of the room was a pair of windows flanked by white eyelet curtains. There was a charming antique secretary that was flanked by two oak bookcases, and a tiled fireplace. A mauve-colored love seat was conveniently situated between the fireplace and the windows.

Back in the bedroom, Laura paused to plump up a pillow then moved on to a set of sliding doors. "There's a lot of closet space," she said, pushing open the doors.

Peering into the closet, Andrea concluded that her wardrobe would take up no more than a third of the space.

"The rooms were just redecorated," Laura said over her shoulder as she went to open the windows. "The last tutor, Miss Cunningham, requested the changes. She gave her notice a week after the remodeling was finished."

Andrea pretended to inspect the view, but she didn't miss the sparkle of amusement in Laura's eyes. "I can't say I'm not glad that Miss Cunningham asked for renovations."

Beside her, Laura laughed. Out the window Andrea caught a glimpse of the footpath that led to the stable barn. The sharp scent of pine needles, blended with the almost indetectable odor of the sea, seeped into the room.

"Salt air's good for the body," Nanna would declare whenever she and Andrea went for a walk along the beach. *"Good for the spirit, too, Andy,"* she'd whisper as she put her arm around her granddaughter.

Andrea drew in a deep breath. A bird twittered in some nearby tree; the pine branches soughed sleepily in the breeze. A fly buzzed by the open window. They were common, everyday sounds. "Is the ocean visible from the house?"

"Just from the Raven's Roost," Laura responded. "It's the only part of Ravenspire that was built high enough to have a view over the tops of the trees."

All at once the sunshine seemed slightly tarnished. Andrea looked up and saw a thin rim of clouds above the trees. She thought of the mysterious windows of the tower and pictured the old woman standing at one of those blank panes, staring sullenly out on her own private view of the Pacific.

Abruptly, Laura turned away from the window. "It's getting late. Let me show you the bath."

The bath was an odd mix of modern and ancient. The vanity, with its brightly illuminated mirror and faux marble top, looked brand new, while the claw-footed tub, with its brass-handled spigots, appeared to be a good match to the sink in the downstairs water closet. Andrea came to the conclusion that it was an agreeable arrangement. She had no complaints about her suite.

Laura accompanied her as far as the foyer, then she left Andrea with the reminder, "Mr. Carraday will be expecting you in his study."

A few minutes later, Andrea entered the study, her signed contract in hand.

Holt took the sheet of paper from her and quickly looked it over. "Good. Everything's in order," he said, rising from his chair. He picked up a miniature ship that was displayed on an Edwardian table and examined it. "When you come back, I'd like for you to take some time to get better acquainted with Elizabeth before you begin formal instruction. I guess that was a mistake on my part in the past. That is . . ." He frowned as he held the ship close and inspected the tiny sails. "I'm afraid that I didn't recognize the importance of first establishing the quality of trust between teacher and pupil."

"Trust should be the foundation of all relationships, don't you think?"

"Yes . . . of course." He set the ship aside. "If there's nothing more, I'll walk you—"

A jangling noise cut short his words. Andrea hadn't noticed the slender black phone that sat unobtrusively on his desk.

A look of annoyance flashed over Holt's features as the phone rang a second time. He lifted the receiver.

"I can find my way out," she said, intent on sparing him the need for an apology.

He nodded and she heard him answer the call as she walked away. His words had a weary ring to them. "The eighteenth through the twentieth? Let me check my calendar."

Starting down the corridor, with its doors shut tight, Andrea might have been traveling the marbled hallways of some ancient, forgotten basilica. The hairs at the back of her neck suddenly prickled, and she had the feeling that she wasn't alone after all. She turned expectantly, assuming that Holt had finished his conversation and was coming to join her. But when she saw the tall figure dressed in black standing just outside the study, watching her, a chill swept through her veins, and her heart gave a slam in her chest.

Andrea quickened her pace. Still, Jayne Evernham's cold gaze snapped at her heels until she came to the end of the corridor. Just before she stepped into the foyer, Andrea cast a furtive glance back. The old woman was gone, vanished like a silent, cloistered monk into some secret chamber.

Chapter Five

A week later, Andrea stood in the middle of her bedroom at Ravenspire, staring in bewilderment at the mound of boxes that surrounded her. Why hadn't her possessions created such a formidable mass stacked in the middle of her empty living room in Boston? Even after hanging her clothes in the spacious closet and putting away her toiletries in the vanity of the adjoining bathroom, the pile in front of her seemed hardly reduced at all.

The move itself had gone more smoothly than she could have hoped for. She'd sold her furniture and her car for a very good price to one of her former colleagues at the academy. And she had thought at the time that she'd done a terrific job of paring down her belongings, eliminating everything but what she considered the necessities.

Her eyes were drawn to the huge trunk that sat beside the bookcase. Taking her keys from her purse, she went to the trunk and opened it. Had she really needed to ship her entire collection of mystery novels across the country? She smiled, recalling her unsuccessful attempt to weed out some of the books. In the end, she'd decided that her collections of Agatha Christie and Arthur Conan Doyle and Mary Higgins Clark were every bit as important to her as her encyclopedias, grammar textbooks, and the classics and poetry anthologies she'd kept since childhood. Yarns of murder and mayhem spun by tough-talking gumshoes seemed an unlikely complement to fairy tales about princesses and unicorns.

Then again, maybe they were. Fairy tales had their share

of spilled blood, too. And a happy ending wasn't the requisite of every childhood story.

As she began to pull books from the trunk, Andrea wondered what kind of stories Elizabeth liked to read. She hoped to soon find out.

On her return to Ravenspire, she'd learned from Laura that Mr. Carraday was gone on another trip, and she'd remembered the phone call he'd received in his study as she prepared to leave for Boston. "The eighteenth through the twentieth?" he'd said wearily into the receiver. Today was the eighteenth.

He'd left behind a brief note addressed to "Miss Lane," which she'd read the moment she found herself alone in her rooms. The note advised her to take a couple of days for unpacking and settling in. But she decided that some of her unpacking could wait. She was more anxious to see Elizabeth, and she intended to spend at least part of the afternoon with the girl.

Andrea looked at the titles she had scattered on the floor in front of her. There was a hardcover edition of Higgins Clark's *While My Pretty One Sleeps*, dog-eared paperbacks of Ellery Queen's *Face to Face* and *Calamity Town*, and a handsome, gilt-edged copy of Christie's *Three Blind Mice and Other Stories*. That was one she hadn't read in a while, she thought, setting it apart from the other books.

She wasn't certain how many books she had in the trunk, but it was a sure bet she couldn't fit all of them into the bookcases. But then it might not be a wise move to put every murder mystery she ever owned on open display. What would her employer think if he happened to see her collection? Well, he had his own quirky interest—his model ships—didn't he?

Andrea took another book from the trunk. *The Hound of the Baskervilles*. The story was Doyle's masterpiece, as far as she was concerned, and one of the spookiest stories she'd ever read. She laid that book aside, too, then rose and went over to the window where she peered out on a dismal view of lawn and sky.

A single raindrop pelted the glass. It was followed by another. The clouds looked threatening, promising a downpour before night. Watching the raindrops splatter against the pane, Andrea considered the prospect of having dinner with Jayne Evernham. The idea held about as much appeal as the notion of tramping the bleak British moors with Mr. Holmes in search of the fiendish hound of the Baskervilles.

Andrea had to laugh at herself. Maybe she'd read a few too many detective stories over the years. For all her overbearing manner, Jayne Evernham wasn't a mad, ghoulish hound—though clad in her long black dress, prowling through the halls of Ravenspire, she bore a similarly ominous presence.

Turning her back to the window, Andrea told herself she was making a mountain out of a molehill. Wasn't it possible that her own anxiousness to win Elizabeth's confidence was causing her to see the old woman as more of a threat than she actually was? She couldn't help but feel an immediate sense of empathy toward the girl, since she had lost her mother at a young age. Like Elizabeth, she'd coped by locking away memories of her mother that proved hurtful to her. Wasn't she still locking away hurtful memories, even if they were of a different sort?

When she'd left Boston, she had purposely discarded anything that might serve as a reminder of Alan and the nightmarish events that shadowed her life the past year. Severing all visible ties with her father would be far more difficult, perhaps impossible, even though she hadn't seen him in over a year and feared she might never see him again.

Andrea went through to the bedroom to her large Pullman case and drew out the fine leather belt she had tucked away in one of the side pockets. The belt had been a gift from her father three years ago. Though it was the wrong size, she'd kept it, believing that it might be the last memento she would ever have of him. She hadn't the heart to ask him if he'd saved the receipt or where she might exchange the belt for one that would fit her. She'd doubted he would be able to recall when or where he'd bought the gift.

Of course, she had the books he'd given her when she was a young girl—fat picture books of beloved nursery rhymes and her favorite, Robert Louis Stevenson's *A Child's Garden of Verses*. She read the Stevenson book so much that it was nearly in tatters. But she wouldn't give it up. She wouldn't give up any of them.

But then she viewed her father differently than she did Alan. She had forgiven her father, come to realize that his gradual slide into self-destruction was a tragedy, the sad consequence of never having found the strength to cope with the fact of his wife's death. She realized now that his decline wasn't somehow her fault and that it hadn't happened because he didn't want her in his life or love her for the person she was.

Alan, on the other hand, she'd finally acknowledged, didn't love her for the person she was, but for the person he perceived her to be in his mind. She thought painfully of how he had tried to mold her into that image—and of how for too long she had allowed him to manipulate her in subtle and not-so-subtle ways. It was his suggestion that she replace her glasses with contacts.

"For heaven's sake, Andrea," he'd said, "why are you hiding those gorgeous eyes behind Coke-bottle lenses?" It was his demand that she cut her hair and have it sculpted into a chic style when she preferred wearing it long and loose. "You're twenty-three, Andrea, a woman, not a schoolgirl," he had chided.

Somehow he'd made her think that he knew what was right for her, that he would always look after her and guide her through life. And she had wanted so badly to believe that he had her best interests at heart. Now she knew how truly naive she'd been.

She ran her hand over the supple brown leather of the belt. It was ironic. She had always admired Alan for his ability to handle any situation with an efficient air of total control. Until she'd been shocked into accepting that he was a conceited jerk, the worst kind of heel. She rolled the belt into a tight coil and stashed it in a drawer of the bureau. Then she reached for the large jewelry box that was propped against her travel case.

She'd just begun to separate two necklace chains that had gotten twisted together when a knock came at the door and Laura called to her. Tossing the necklaces aside, she went to answer the door.

The housekeeper stepped into the room, holding a covered tray in her hands. "Sybil and I thought you'd probably want to have your lunch up here today." She looked around. "I see you're making progress. But you must be tired. Can't I help in some way?"

Ever the diplomat, decided Andrea of the housekeeper, though she'd assured Laura earlier that she preferred doing her own unpacking. "Thanks, but I think I'll take a break this afternoon. I'd like to spend some time getting acquainted with Elizabeth."

The housekeeper walked through the archway and set the tray on the table by the love seat. "I'll make sure Elizabeth's in her rooms after lunch," she said with her usual gracious air.

An hour later, Andrea stood in front of Elizabeth's closed door. A small tremor of anticipation raced up her spine as she knocked. It was the same feeling she'd always gotten on the first day of a new school year at the academy.

It was Laura, not Elizabeth, who came to the door and directed her inside.

Andrea noted that the girl's suite was similar to her own combination bed and sitting room, though not as spacious. There was a four-poster bed without a canopy. Its lacy comforter sported a colorful splash of pink and yellow flowers. A number of frilly pillows flanked by dolls and assorted stuffed animals graced the head end of the bed while a brass trunk stood at the foot end. The length of one wall was taken up by shelves crammed with more dolls and various toys.

Though there was a small television and VCR sandwiched in the top shelf between dolls and jigsaw puzzles, missing were the requisite computer and video games and other electronic gadgetry that Andrea had been accustomed to seeing in the kids' dorms at the academy. Otherwise, the room could have been any young girl's room.

"In here," Laura said.

They went through the archway into the other, smaller room. Andrea was pleased to see that it was a classroom complete with blackboard, various maps, and several math and grammar charts. A large polished wood desk, obviously the tutor's, stood in front of a bare window, while a child-size desk was situated at right angles nearby. A filing cabinet occupied one corner of the room; a globe of the world on a high pedestal was set in another. Books and boxes, whose contents were hidden, spilled over the shelves that were built into the wall under the window. The odor of chalk dust hung in the air.

"Elizabeth?" the housekeeper called out. She walked behind the desk and motioned for Andrea to join her.

The girl was sitting cross-legged in front of the shelves, her curly blond head bent over the pieces of a jigsaw puzzle that was spread out on the floor.

"Miss Lane's here to see you," Laura said, crouching beside the girl.

Elizabeth reached across Laura and grabbed a tiny piece of puzzle. She held it up for inspection.

Andrea knelt on the other side of Laura. She watched the girl's hands work to fit the piece to the several that were already joined together.

"This is the castle in the Magic Kingdom," Elizabeth said without looking up.

"The puzzle's one of your favorites, isn't it?" Laura put in.

"Dad promised we'd go to Disney World in Florida."

Laura sent Andrea a sideways glance. "And I'm sure you will as soon as he can find the time."

Elizabeth frowned, and Andrea wondered how long the girl had been waiting for her dad to fulfill his promise.

"Why don't we put the Magic Kingdom aside for now, Elizabeth, and show Miss Lane around."

With a sigh, the girl dropped the puzzle piece and got up from the floor. She peered at Andrea through thick silver-blond lashes. After a moment, she asked, "Have you ever been to Florida?"

"No, never, but I'd like to someday."

Elizabeth walked to a map of the United States and Canada. "Dad said you're from Boston." She correctly pointed out the city on the map. "I've been to New York," she said, again hitting the correct spot with her finger. "And Toronto and Vancouver." She stretched on her toes to indicate the Canadian cities.

"You know your geography well," Andrea said.

"Elizabeth's an excellent student," Laura offered with a touch of pride.

They moved on from the map to examine the shelves of books. The lower shelf was crammed with a wide variety of textbooks, a complete set of encyclopedias, and boxes of flash cards and other study aids. There were fiction books, too. Classics such as *Charlotte's Web*, Kipling's *Just So Stories*, and *A Little Princess* shared space with more current titles such as *Freckle Juice* and *Hannah's Fancy Notions*. It appeared that Holt didn't stint when it came to providing a wealth of reading material for his daughter.

"I have some of the same titles in my own collection," Andrea said, selecting an anthology of children's poetry.

A bit of Elizabeth's reserve seemed to slip away as she reached out to touch the book. "Dad used to read poems to me sometimes when I was little," she said.

Over the girl's head, Andrea exchanged smiles with Laura.

"Well," Laura said, "if you two will excuse me, I've got cleaning to catch up on."

Andrea met the housekeeper's eyes. "Thank you," she said, grateful that Laura had been there to smooth the way with Elizabeth. But now that Laura was leaving, Andrea felt the "beginning-of-school jitters" overcoming her again. She told herself to be patient, that friendships weren't forged in a day. Wasn't that why Holt had requested she take a period of time to get to know his daughter before beginning formal instruction?

Following the girl around the classroom, asking discreet questions, Andrea concluded that she'd taught kids who were far more shy than Elizabeth. But the exquisite face with its expressive eyes had a haunting quality about it that again made Andrea aware she was dealing with more than a case of reticence. It was as if she were seeing herself at eight years old, a child stricken with grief and confusion over the loss of her mother, precocious and wise in some ways, uncertain and immature in others.

There was another thing Andrea noticed as Elizabeth introduced her to her favorite dolls, Mrs. Muffin and Miss Violet. There was only one photograph in the girl's suite, as far as Andrea could tell—a candid shot of Holt standing alone beside a tree. He was dressed in jeans and riding boots and a white sweater, and his hair looked as if the wind had been blowing through it. He wasn't smiling for the camera. There were no pictures of father and daughter together, as Andrea might have expected. And none of Victoria Carraday. Was it because, as Holt had said, Elizabeth recalled little of her mother?

"We don't have cable," Elizabeth said, skipping over to the television. She punched the on/off button. A dim picture flickered onto the screen then went out.

"Do you ever watch videos?" Andrea asked.

"Sometimes," Elizabeth said with a sigh. "I like *Aladdin* and *Beauty and the Beast*. Dad bought me *The Little Mermaid*. I have a mermaid doll." She went to a shelf and returned with the doll. "I'd rather ride Patches than watch TV or movies," she said, twisting the doll in her hands.

"I thought maybe we could go riding tomorrow. Would you show me your favorite trails?"

The girl's eyes lit up. Then she turned and went to place the doll where it belonged on the shelf. When she came back, she swung her arms in a restless manner. "I'm hungry," she said, staring out the window. "But Auntie Jayne says we have to wait until six to eat because that's the proper dinner hour."

Chapter Six

"Shoulders straight, Elizabeth."

At Jayne Evernham's command to the girl, Andrea hunched lower in her chair. *Don't cower,* she told herself, and sat erect again.

"Auntie Jayne" had been correcting Elizabeth ever since they'd sat down to dinner, provoking in Andrea a rising tide of sympathy for the girl and disdain for the old woman. "Not that fork, Elizabeth, the other one for the salad," Jayne chided with a bony finger pointed in the girl's direction. "The napkin will do you no good if you don't put it to proper use," she scolded, dabbing at the corners of her floridly made-up mouth with her own napkin.

Andrea watched in dismay as Elizabeth gobbled her food. She couldn't imagine how the child was able to eat a single forkful under the circumstances. Or how Holt Carraday could tolerate his aunt's behavior for one day longer. Was it possible that "Auntie Jayne" was overplaying her role to impress the new tutor, whom she clearly looked down on, and to send another silent message that the tutor was not welcome at Ravenspire?

"A lady does not stuff her mouth," Jayne intoned. "A lady eats like this." She demonstrated, delicately bringing a forkful of salad to the red-painted lips. As she chewed the bite, a trickle of French dressing oozed from her mouth and dribbled down her jutting chin.

Repulsed by the sight, Andrea took a long sip from her water glass and fixed her eyes on a candle burning in its brass holder. She heard Jayne sawing through her piece of steak.

On the other side of her, Elizabeth gave a heaving sigh and began to tap her fork against her plate.

Tap. Tap. "I'm full, Auntie Jayne." *Tap. Tap. Tap.* "Can I be excused?"

"*May* is the correct word. And you *may not* be excused because you haven't finished your meal."

Andrea half expected Jayne to mention the hungry children in South America or China.

"I don't feel well." *Tap. Tap.*

"Clever excuse." The old woman reached over and snatched the fork out of the girl's hand. "Off to bed, and we'll not hear another peep from you until morning."

Elizabeth pushed back her chair and shot from the room. Andrea stared after her, wishing she could dash away, too.

The silence was deafening. From outside the mansion came a distant rumble of thunder, then the sound of rain hitting the windows. Andrea brought a bite of steak to her mouth and chewed without tasting the meat. She sensed that Jayne was studying her, calculating how many hours or days would pass before the new tutor made her meek and nervous departure from the mansion.

Finally, Jayne cleared her throat. "He took down all the pictures of her, you know."

Andrea froze, her fork poised in midair. She gave Jayne the barest glance, determined not to say the word "who."

"I thought you might wonder why you haven't seen any portraits of Mrs. Carraday at Ravenspire."

A streak of lightning briefly illumined the dark panes of glass. Setting her fork aside, Andrea made herself look at Jayne. "No," she fibbed.

"Oh, come," the old woman said with an impatient thrust of her bony hand. "Victoria was an actress on the British stage. Tall, elegant, very beautiful, of course. The embodiment of sophistication. My nephew has a weakness for beautiful women." The sharp blue eyes narrowed. "But that isn't hard to guess, is it, Miss Lane?"

"Really, Mrs. Evernham, I don't consider it any of my

business to concern myself with the affairs of Mr. Carraday and his . . . late wife.''

"Now isn't it human nature to be curious?" The old woman blotted her mouth on her napkin; the ruby red lipstick smeared outside the line of her lips.

"Holt would never admit how many women have fallen victim to his charms," Jayne went on. "Doubtless he takes after his father for his allure. What a wicked charmer Kenton Carraday was." She leaned her black-clad arms on the table and stared at Andrea from her skull white face. "It came as no surprise to me that Holt had one thought on his mind when he met Victoria—to wed her as quickly as possible. Now he lives in his own private torment. Victoria sealed his fate when she died, and he will never be free from the memory of her. *Never,*" Jayne said, her voice dropping to a whisper.

The blood pounded in Andrea's temples. The sight of the half-eaten piece of steak, the mound of duchess potatoes, nauseated her. She pushed back her chair and, with all the control she could muster, said, "Excuse me, but I have unpacking to do."

"Oh well, tomorrow evening then, Miss Lane. Have a restful night."

There was an undertone of mocking in the harsh voice, and Andrea sensed this was the moment Jayne had been waiting for—to be able to revel in the triumph of knowing she had put the new tutor in an embarrassing position. Andrea made no response, only turned and walked away from the table in as dignified a manner as possible.

The next morning, Andrea drove the Toyota into Seacliff and opened a bank account with the money she'd received for her furniture and car. Holt had been as good as his word, having had new tires put on the Toyota, and Andrea was pleased to discover that the car ran at least as well as her former Civic.

Having reliable transportation at her disposal gave Andrea a measure of confidence in another way. Whenever she felt the need to escape the confines of Ravenspire—and the company of Jayne Evernham at the dinner table—all she need do was jump in the Toyota and take off. And the knowledge that she had a small nest egg in the bank gave her a certain sense of security. Though she had never been a quitter, if conditions warranted it in the future, she could always follow the lead of the former tutors and make her exit, knowing she had at least enough money to tide her over for a couple of months while she sought other employment—or to finance a trip back east to the academy's campus in Maine, if all else failed.

As she pulled into the parking lot of The Timbers Café, her stomach gave a growl, reminding her that she'd skipped breakfast because she'd overslept by a half hour. On going downstairs, she had made up an excuse to Sybil about having errands to run in Seacliff.

The night before, Jayne's revelation about her nephew had followed Andrea into sleep, and she had dreamed of Holt. She had dreamed of Alan, too, a troubling vision where she was his wife, and he was taunting her. *"You think I married you because I love you, Andrea? Silly woman. You're my grand experiment, my little success story. I made you what you are."* His eyes narrowed. *"And I'm never going to let you forget it."*

She'd wakened with a gasp to find the covers on her bed were a tangled mess, evidence of her tossing and turning. Hands shaking in silent rage, she had cursed Alan for his callousness. She had wanted his respect and love. But she had also wanted to be cherished—perhaps more desperately than she had been willing to admit. And he had taken advantage of her need.

Was Holt Carraday as shallow as Alan Grimes? she'd asked herself in the darkness. Had Victoria been Holt's little trophy, his success story turned sour?

What should I care about Holt's personal life? Andrea thought as she pushed open the door to the café. Whether he lived a life of torment—or of unbounded happiness—was of no consequence to her. He was a wealthy businessman. She was his daughter's tutor. That was the extent of their relationship, wasn't it? Then why did she feel inexplicably drawn to him, and why did he haunt her dreams at night?

Andrea was disappointed when she saw no sign of Maggie in the crowded café. Instead, a gum-chewing blond with a surly expression steered Andrea to a booth and took her order with an air of bored efficiency. When she asked the waitress about Maggie, the response was a curt, "It's her day off." Other than that, the only comment Andrea managed to extract from the woman was that Seacliff's beach was "a bummer," and not worth the bother of a visit.

Discounting the waitress's advice, Andrea left her car parked at a meter and walked the several blocks to the beach, a pebbly strip of shore that snaked north of Seacliff's boat dock and pier. There were a few unpainted benches where one could sit on a more favorable day and enjoy the view. But the benches were empty that morning, and the rollers had a gray, angry appearance as they spat their foam on the shore.

The beach was a disappointment, Andrea had to admit. It was nothing like the wide, sandy stretch of shore that she used to look out on from Nanna's back porch in Oregon. Gazing at the sky, she saw a pair of seagulls wheeling above her, hoping for a handout. She had nothing to offer them, not even a crumb. With a sigh, she slid her hands in the pockets of her jacket and headed up the beach toward her car.

"Do you believe in ghosts, Miss Lane?"

Andrea picked up a piece of jigsaw puzzle and studied for a moment where it might fit into the Magic Kingdom. "No, I don't, Elizabeth," she said.

"Dad doesn't either." The girl's lips pursed in a frown. "I asked him once."

Andrea looked up. "Do you believe in them, Elizabeth?"

The girl appeared to be deeply concentrating on her puzzle piece. "I think maybe that Auntie Jayne does," she said at last.

Andrea grew alert. "Did she say that to you?"

"Not exactly."

"What makes you think she believes in ghosts?"

"Because..." Elizabeth bit her lip. "She tells me stories."

"About ghosts?"

"No, but about other scary things. She told me one last night."

"Didn't you go upstairs right after dinner?"

Elizabeth nodded. "Sometimes Auntie Jayne comes into my room when I'm in bed. She sits in the chair."

"Which chair?"

Elizabeth got up, the puzzle piece still in her hand, and led Andrea through the archway from the classroom to her bedroom. She pointed at a rocking chair set in a corner near the bed. "This one," she said.

Andrea hadn't noticed the chair before. "Do you remember the story Mrs. Evernham told you last night?" she asked, sitting down on the edge of the bed.

Elizabeth sat in the rocker. The chair dwarfed her petite frame; her feet didn't come close to touching the floor. "There was a man—a very selfish and *evil* man," she began, her gaze fixed on an invisible spot on the wall, "who lived in a huge castle by the sea. He had no wife because she died, and no one from the village came to visit him because the people were afraid of him. They said that when there was a full moon, the man turned into a terrible, fierce bird who roamed the skies over the woods near his castle. If anyone was foolish enough to go out in the moonlight, the bird would capture them with his sharp talons and take them to the castle and throw them into the dungeon where it's pitch black and they couldn't see even their fingers or their toes in front of them. The man-bird kept them locked in his dungeon until they died and became skeletons."

A chill spread through Andrea as she recalled her dreams of Holt and the raven. Observing Elizabeth, she saw that the girl's face was set in an almost trancelike pose. "Is there more?" Andrea prompted.

Elizabeth turned the puzzle piece over and over in her hands. "Auntie Jayne said there was one little girl, more foolish and naughty than the all the rest, who didn't believe the story about the man. So she went to visit the castle by the sea. And as she passed through the dark woods, she thought, 'this is nice, the moon is shining; there's nothing to fear.' Then all at once, a huge bird came out of the sky and snatched her up and carried her off to the castle. The bird turned back into the man, and he threw the girl in the dungeon and never let her go."

"That sounds very scary," Andrea said softly. *Even more so,* she thought, *because Jayne is the one who told you the story.* "Is that the end?"

"No," Elizabeth said in a small tremulous voice. "Auntie Jayne said *I* was the girl. She said that *I* . . ." Elizabeth's lower lip began to quiver.

Andrea moved forward at the same time that Elizabeth reached for her. Her arms came around Elizabeth. "What did Mrs. Evernham say?"

Elizabeth gazed up. Her eyes were wide and shining. "She said that I must be good and *always* listen to her and never act naughty because the man will snatch me up. I dreamed that he came for me, and I woke up and saw the bird at the window. Then I pulled the covers tight over my head and didn't look out again until morning."

"It's all right," Andrea soothed. "It was just a story, Elizabeth. People can't change into animals and hurt you." Inwardly, she was outraged at Jayne. And angry at Holt. Did he have any idea of the unwholesome influence his aunt was having on his daughter? Did he want to know? Or was he content to wallow in his own troubles?

You're not being fair to him, Andrea told herself. Maybe he didn't realize the harm Jayne was doing. But he'd learn soon enough because Andrea was going to be the one to inform him about the old woman's behavior.

"Miss Lane?"

"Yes, Elizabeth?" She felt the girl beginning to relax.

"Could we finish the puzzle now?"

"Yes, I think we should."

They went back into the classroom and sat on the floor. But somehow the Magic Kingdom had lost its appeal, and it was with only halfhearted enthusiasm that they fitted the last pieces into place.

Elizabeth sat still, staring at the finished puzzle for a moment. Then she went to her desk and returned with a sheaf of papers which she handed to Andrea.

They were drawings—the first one was of a pony and was labeled PATCHES in neat printing at the bottom; the second was a colored scene of trees and blue sky and sun. Andrea was impressed. "Did you draw these, Elizabeth?"

"Uh-huh."

Andrea leafed through the rest. There were two more of Patches, one of a man who was obviously Holt, though it wasn't labeled as such, and another of a slender, blond-haired woman wearing a flowered dress. Andrea guessed the woman was Laura, though it wasn't an accurate likeness. At least there weren't any pictures of frightening birds or dungeons. "These are very good," she said.

"Dad said Grandma Carraday was an artist."

"Then you inherited your talent from her. I saw the portrait of Ravenspire that your grandmother painted."

"She died before I was born."

"Yes, I know." Andrea waited, hoping by some slim chance Elizabeth might mention her mother.

The moment passed, and Andrea handed the drawings back to the girl. Checking her watch, she saw it was a quarter to six. According to "Auntie Jayne," the proper dinner hour was six. As she went to her rooms to freshen up, Andrea thought of the story Elizabeth had told her, and she wondered what kind of bizarre dreams Jayne Evernham had at night.

"Passion drove Holt to marry her, not love."

It had begun again. Throughout dinner, Andrea had observed how Jayne was chomping at the bit for Elizabeth to leave so that she could start in on the new tutor. Now that the girl had finished her meal and gone upstairs, the old woman had free rein.

"You've seen the ballet *Swan Lake,* Miss Lane?"

"Yes, of course."

"Victoria was another Odette—graceful, lovely, swanlike in appearance," Jayne crooned. "That is, until Holt brought her to this wretched place."

Andrea almost choked on her water as she realized that *Swan Lake*—or rather a convoluted version of it—was the story Jayne had told Elizabeth the night before. "Then you view your nephew as the evil von Rothbart?" she asked.

The old woman's eyes narrowed. "I assure you that Holt can play the part of the enchanter very well."

"In the ballet," Andrea said, ignoring Jayne's comment, "von Rothbart's curse is broken when the noble Prince Siegfried throws himself into the lake after Odette."

"Precisely, Miss Lane. Precisely." Jayne suddenly sagged back in her chair. She looked shrunken, her eyes glazed over, as if she too had fallen under a spell. After a while, she resumed eating but with the mechanical motions of an automaton. She paid no more attention to Andrea than if she weren't there at all, though on occasion she made some random gesture and muttered words to herself.

Finally, Andrea got up and left the dining room without the usual sensation that Jayne's eyes were following her.

The sun came out the next morning. Except for a slight briskness in the air, it was a perfect Indian summer day. Andrea gladly welcomed the change in the weather, and after breakfast, she and Elizabeth set off for the stable barn.

Carl saddled up Patches and Shadow and walked them out of their stalls to the end of the barn where Andrea and Elizabeth waited. When Andrea thanked him, he touched his cap in acknowledgment, but his face reflected skepticism, and she guessed he was doubting that she knew how to mount a horse. She quickly demonstrated that she had the capability.

Elizabeth announced that they would take the Raven's Route first because it was her favorite trail. As they started down the winding path that originated behind the barn, Andrea was bound to observe how at home and confident the young girl looked on the pony. There was hardly a trace of the wide-eyed, apprehensive child who had confided to Andrea that "Auntie Jayne" sat in the rocker at night and spun scary stories.

With Elizabeth in the lead, they explored the entire length of the Raven's Route, an overgrown and twisted trail flanked by thick brush and vines. Occasionally the trail was intersected by another, which Elizabeth identified as West Trail. The odor of salt in the air grew stronger the farther they rode, and Andrea guessed the trail wound very near the water. The Raven's Route came to an abrupt end where a narrow footpath began.

"Dad told me never to climb up the rocks," Elizabeth said with a glance back, "because it's dangerous."

Andrea rode up beside the girl. "What rocks are those?"

"The ones at the end of the path." Elizabeth pointed. "Auntie Jayne said the Indians carved the steps in the rocks so they could punish people who were bad by throwing them off the cliffs and into the ocean."

A shadow fell across the trail. Gazing at the sky, Andrea saw that a small cloud covered the sun. Were the cliffs that the girl spoke of the ones where Victoria had fallen—or leaped—to her death?

"I'd hope," Andrea said, "that the Indians would have had a better reason for carving stairs out of stone than to use them for tossing people into the ocean."

Elizabeth turned Patches around and took the lead once more. Though they explored West Trail and another named Ivy Fork Trail, neither one held the same fascination that the Raven's Route did for Andrea, and she decided that she would come back another day when she was alone and climb up the stone steps to see the rocks for herself.

When Andrea returned to the house, she learned from

Laura that Holt was home from his trip. She requested through Laura to speak with him at his earliest convenience, and the housekeeper relayed back a message from Mr. Carraday that she was to come to his study that evening after dinner.

Andrea anticipated that Holt would eat with them in the dining room. But he didn't show. To Andrea's relief, Jayne appeared distracted and disinclined toward conversation of any sort, and the meal had passed without the usual barrage of criticism over Elizabeth's table manners. Still, Andrea barely tasted her food, her mind on the approaching meeting with Holt. After beating a quick retreat to her rooms to freshen up, she went downstairs to the study.

Holt was sitting at his desk. At Andrea's entrance, he got up from his chair and waited until she came forward.

He was dressed as she was, casually, in slacks and a sweater. The slacks were of a rich-looking tweed material and the burgundy shade of his fisherman's knit sweater set off his gleaming black hair and enhanced the lean, strong column of his neck.

"Miss Lane." He gestured for her to sit in the upholstered chair.

As she settled herself, she noticed that the top of his desk was littered with pieces of wood, snippets of paper and wire, and various small tools and brushes. In the hearth, a fire burned, diminishing the damp chill that always seemed to permeate the mansion.

"*The HMY Portsmouth,*" Holt said, holding up a miniature ship that was in an advanced stage of construction. "What do you think?"

"It's . . . very nice," she said.

Holt cocked an eyebrow. "Nice?" He picked up a tiny pair of pliers and clamped them around a wire that secured a portion of the sail to the deck.

"Perhaps handsome is a better word," she replied, watching his hands as he gave the wire a fast twist with the pliers.

"Can you guess what the sails are made of?" he asked.

"Some type of cloth . . . cotton, maybe?"

"Actually, it's rice paper that's been given a coat of diluted brown watercolor. As the paint dries, crinkling occurs, which will help give the finished sails a realistic appearance. The sails are cut from the paper with a razor blade, fitted with knots and jackstays and . . ." He laughed. "Excuse me," he said, setting the ship and pliers aside, "you didn't come here to listen to a lecture on how to construct a fake sail."

No, she thought, *I certainly didn't.* But she also didn't want to appear impolite. "Have you been building ships for a long time?"

"Five years." He looked away, picked up a piece of rice paper and a small paintbrush. "Is there a problem with my daughter?"

"Not *with* your daughter, Mr. Carraday. She's delightful to be around, and I'm very pleased with the progress we've made in getting to know each other. But I'm concerned about something she mentioned to me the other day."

He regarded her expectantly.

"Elizabeth said that . . . Mrs. Evernham comes into her room at night and tells her frightening stories—stories that cause Elizabeth to have nightmares."

Holt set the paintbrush aside. "How long has this been going on?" he asked.

"Elizabeth didn't say, but I suspect that it's been a while. She wanted to know if I believe in ghosts."

"Do you?" Holt asked, picking up the brush again. He dipped the brush in a jar of brown paint and made a succession of deft strokes with the brush across the rice paper.

"Of course not," Andrea retorted. "But I can't help noticing the influence that Mrs. Evernham has over your daughter and . . ." *In for a penny, in for a pound.* "From what I've observed at the dinner table, your aunt has Elizabeth afraid to make a move out of fear that she's done something wrong and that . . . her aunt is going to punish her. Elizabeth picks at her food and runs off before she's half finished eating."

Suddenly, as if he hadn't been listening, Holt threw the

brush down and wadded the piece of rice paper in his hand. "That's ruined," he said, tossing the balled-up paper aside. He rose from his chair and paced to the hearth.

Andrea was stung by his actions. Though his back was turned to her so that she couldn't see his expression, she noted the rigid set of his shoulders, the stiff movement of his arm as he brought his hand to rest on the mantel. She got up and went to stand behind him. The clock ticked loudly in her ears as she waited for Holt to speak.

"I had no idea," he said finally, his voice muffled.

"I'm not surprised. How could you possibly know what's going on here when you're away all the time?" She hurled the question at his back without thinking.

Holt wheeled around to face her, nearly throwing her off balance. Their gazes locked combatively for a moment.

Here it comes, Andrea thought. *He's going to fire me.* She didn't care. If he had no more regard for his daughter than he'd displayed in the last few minutes, he would be doing the new tutor a favor by dismissing her.

But his eyes broke contact with hers. His shoulders slumped visibly, and he sank down in one of the two upholstered chairs that were set near the hearth. He gestured for Andrea to take the other chair. Clenching his hands together, he stared into the fire. "You may have difficulty believing this," he said, "but I do love my daughter."

Andrea kept silent because she wasn't sure, in all honesty, that she wouldn't question his statement. Then he turned his head slightly, and she caught the look of bewilderment and sadness etched on his face. A stab of grief tore through her heart. She knew that look, had seen it a thousand times in her father's eyes.

"And I've been away too much," he admitted, running a hand through his hair. "I suppose part of the problem is that I've felt"—he seemed to grope for the right words—"in a quandary over how I might . . . fill the void in my daughter's life left by her mother's death."

Holt looked so miserable that Andrea suddenly ached to

reach out to him—just as she had often wanted to reach out to her father—to reassure him in some way.

Remember that some hurts can't be healed, she told herself. "I don't think the void that's left when a loved ones dies can ever really be filled," she said. "Nor should we expect ourselves to try to fill it."

"Maybe not," he hesitantly agreed, "but I'm afraid it's more complicated than that. There were certain . . . questions about my wife's death to which I've never found satisfactory answers. I doubt now that I ever will."

He lapsed into silence, and Andrea remembered Jayne's spiteful words. *"Holt lives in torment. . . . Victoria sealed his fate. . . . He will never be free."*

He doesn't believe that Victoria's death was an accident, thought Andrea, *and he's torturing himself—and probably blaming himself—because he can't know for sure.*

Holt lifted his head and squared his shoulders. "Well," he said, his tone almost brusque, "I think the time has come for me to make other living arrangements for my aunt."

Andrea felt an immediate sense of relief. Now that he had committed himself to getting Jayne out of the house, she couldn't help asking, "How did your aunt come to live at Ravenspire?"

"My mother rescued her."

"Rescued?"

Holt's features softened; there was even a glint of amusement in his eyes. "When she was young, Jayne had visions of being a professional dancer. In fact, she performed in cabaret shows and a few musical productions at a theater in Portland. But apparently Stewart Evernham was a possessive man, and after their marriage, he forbade Jayne to set foot on the stage again. I imagine that's why she came to despise me."

"Because her husband wouldn't allow her to dance?"

Holt looked into the fire again. "Because my wife, Victoria, was an actress before we married, and Jayne saw me as the villain who, like her husband, took his wife away from the limelight. Jayne doted on Victoria," he went on. "It was obvious that she felt a kinship with my wife because of their mutual love of the stage. And the feeling seemed to be returned, as far as I could tell. In any case, after Jayne had been married for a number of years, she had illusions of resuming her career. So, she left Stewart. But by then she was nearing forty and past her prime as a dancer. She finally ended up ill and broke, living in a rat-infested boardinghouse in Portland. My mother received a telegram from someone who knew Jayne, and she brought Jayne to Ravenspire."

Holt rose and paced over to a table, where he retrieved a glass-enclosed ship. He polished the glass case with the sleeve of his sweater, then returned to his chair. "That isn't all," he said. "It turned out that Jayne had a head for business. My mother didn't. So when the family pharmaceutical empire was about to collapse, Jayne came to the rescue with some sound financial advice. And when Stewart died, she inherited a tidy sum, part of which she used to help finance my stint at boarding school. Over time, though, Jayne began to keep pretty much to herself. After my mother died, she took up permanent residence in the tower, which she named the Raven's Roost. With Victoria's death, she started dressing in black, as if to remind us that she's in a perpetual state of mourning."

Andrea didn't know what to say. Holt's story had stirred in her a strange sense of sympathy toward Jayne Evernham— the kind of sympathy that one might have for some tragically flawed figure. Though it didn't negate her less charitable feelings toward the old woman, it did add a new dimension to them.

It was a moment before Andrea realized that Holt had moved away from her and walked to his desk. She got up and followed. He picked up the ship model he'd been working on and looked closely at the hull. "This needs more work," he said with impatience. He put the ship aside and threw the crumpled piece of rice paper into a wastebasket beside his desk. "So..."

Their eyes met. Without knowing quite why, Andrea plucked the rice paper from the wastebasket. She laid the paper on the surface of the desk and began to press out the worst creases.

"What are you doing?" he asked.

She smoothed the paper, admiring the little markings Holt had made with the watercolor brush. "Didn't you say crinkling the rice paper gives the sails a realistic effect?"

"Yes, but the markings I made on that piece of paper are flawed."

"I'm no expert," she said, "but the markings look just fine to me. I think this could be a perfectly acceptable sail." She held the paper up to the rigging on the model ship. "There. See?"

For the first time that evening, Holt smiled at her.

"Maybe you're right," he said, taking the paper and ship from her hands. "It might do, after all."

Chapter Seven

The next morning, Andrea learned that Holt had been called away unexpectedly on business—an emergency meeting of the board of his company, Laura believed. He expected to be gone two or three days and would return by Saturday at the latest. As she drank her orange juice and ate her eggs and toast, Andrea told herself she had no reason to feel upset because he'd left again. Hadn't he finally taken seriously her concerns about Jayne's influence over his daughter? And hadn't he indicated that he intended to make other living arrangements for his aunt?

Andrea had to believe that he would be as good as his word in regard to Jayne. But she couldn't seem to forget the memory of the way his gaze had caught and held hers before she left his study the night before. Nor could she ignore the stab of longing that made her remember how much she had wanted to stay and help him polish the wood on the tiny ship he held in his hands, and to hold the crinkled rice paper sail in place while he fitted it to the rigging.

She promptly dismissed her thoughts as foolish and made a promise to herself to try to put Holt out of her mind and concentrate on Elizabeth—which was her reason for being at Ravenspire in the first place.

The weather held over the next couple of days, and Andrea and Elizabeth took full advantage of the sunny skies by spending as much time as possible on the trails. Andrea became familiar with all the places where the Raven's Route and West Trail intersected and which offshoots were false trails that led nowhere.

Andrea discovered that she had misjudged Shadow in comparing her disposition to that of her former mistress. The mare was actually a placid, cooperative animal that seemed to know the trails as well as Elizabeth's pony.

Elizabeth looked happiest when she was on Patches, though her face never quite lost its expression of reticence. It was particularly at those times when they rode the Raven's Route and Elizabeth grew very quiet that Andrea thought about Victoria Carraday and the stone stairs the Indians had carved out of the rocks to carry people to their deaths.

In the evenings at the dinner table, Andrea thought about Victoria, too, and about the fact that she and Elizabeth might not have to bear Jayne's company much longer. For her part, Jayne was unusually subdued, as if she sensed something was up. At times, she would simply sit and stare across the table at Andrea. At other times, she would mumble under her breath to herself, making a grand gesture now and then.

Was Jayne slipping more and more into a world of her own making, blurring reality and illusion? Or was she merely clever and calculating, hoping to unnerve the new tutor and cause her to crack?

Three days passed and there'd been no word of Holt's return. On Saturday, Andrea woke to the rhythm of rain beating on the windows. She had dreamed of a storm driving the rain in from the ocean. She'd dreamed of the blue-eyed raven, too, its impressive wings spread wide as it soared through the darkened sky.

One thing she hadn't dreamed. She'd heard Holt's voice echoing in the hallway the night before as he spoke to someone, perhaps his daughter or Laura. After a moment, there'd been the sound of a door closing, then silence.

Shivering, Andrea went to look out the windows. There was no storm yet, just a nuisance kind of rain and a gusty breeze that shook the panes of glass. She stared at the cold, empty hearth, yearning for a fire to warm her hands.

After plaiting her hair in a braid and putting on slacks and two layers of sweaters, Andrea went downstairs to breakfast.

She saw no sign of either Holt or Elizabeth, so she ate alone, dining on the hot cereal, fresh fruit, and tea that Sybil served her with only the barest nod of recognition.

Andrea was just finishing up a second cup of tea when Laura appeared to inform her that Elizabeth wasn't feeling well and that her father was with her.

"Just a stomach virus, I expect," Laura said. "Mr. Carraday has prescribed bed rest—over Elizabeth's protests, naturally."

"What can I do for her, Laura?"

"Thank you, but there's nothing at the moment, though Elizabeth might want to see you later." Laura paused. "Mr. Carraday did ask me to request that you come to his study for coffee this afternoon. At four o'clock?"

Andrea's fingers tightened around the cup. "Yes, tell him that would be fine."

"Is there anything you need, Andrea?"

"I can't think of . . . Actually, a fire would be nice."

"I'll take care of it." Laura turned to go. "And why don't I bring your lunch up for you, too. I doubt Mr. Carraday will be coming down to eat until evening."

Andrea passed the day curled up on the mauve love seat in front of a crackling fire. She picked up the Christie book that she hadn't read in a while and began with the story *Three Blind Mice*. Any Christie story generally held her interest, but she suddenly found she couldn't concentrate. The nuisance rain had become a full-blown gale, and more than once, Andrea laid the book aside to stare out the window. Watching the streams of water coursing down the glass, she thought about the fact that Holt had invited her for coffee and wondered what his purpose was for asking her.

At noon, Andrea got a progress report on Elizabeth when Laura brought in her lunch.

"Her father coaxed her to eat a small bowl of soup," Laura said. "Then she went back to sleep."

"Tell Elizabeth I asked about her."

"I will," Laura said on her way out.

Ravenspire

The afternoon crept by until finally it was quarter to four. Andrea put on fresh makeup and removed the bands from her braided hair. She shook the curly strands loose, fluffing them with her hands so that they fell free around her shoulders.

Her image in the mirror arrested her attention. *Why am I so concerned about my appearance when all I'm going to do is have coffee with my employer?* Meeting the reflection of her eyes, she couldn't hide the truth from herself. *It's because I want him to see me as pretty, not plain. I want him to be attracted to me.*

A cold knot formed in her stomach and her hands shook as she turned away from her reflection. Holt Carraday attracted to her? Why was she wishing for something that was impossible and ridiculous? Holt was a wealthy man, a compellingly handsome man who could have his pick of women. Perhaps he had already met someone, and that was more the reason he was away from home than tending to business matters. Besides, in her own tentative emotional state, the last thing she needed was for a man still grieving over the circumstances of his wife's death to desire her.

Andrea took several deep breaths to calm herself. Then she walked out the door and down to Holt's study.

"Come in, Miss Lane."

Holt rose from one of the chairs by the hearth. He motioned for her to join him.

"Lousy weather," he said, settling back in his chair.

"Yes," she agreed. "I'm sorry Elizabeth's not feeling well. I missed her."

Holt leaned forward and locked his hands together. The fine patrician nose and high cheekbones stood out in the light cast by the fire. "Elizabeth missed you, too," he said. "By tomorrow she should be back to her old self."

"That's good," Andrea said.

They fell into silence, he staring into the fire, she sliding discreet glances his way. A log broke apart with a shower of sparks. Andrea watched the tiny points of light fade one by one.

Laura came in, carrying a large decorative tray. She placed it on a table beside the two chairs. With a cheerful bustle of activity, she poured coffee from a silver pot into white ceramic mugs. "Cream? Sugar?" she asked Andrea.

"Just black, thank you."

The housekeeper handed Andrea one of the mugs and gave the other to her employer. Then she left.

"Some biscotti with your coffee?" Holt offered Andrea a plate mounded with the Italian cookies. "I see we have a choice of anise or almond-flavored."

Andrea sensed that he was relieved to be occupied with some activity, however small. She chose an almond biscuit, while Holt took an anise one.

"Do you know, Miss Lane, that the first time I tasted biscotti was at an outdoor café in Paris?"

"Really?" she said, taking a bite from her cookie. She saw that Holt was smiling. She hoped he was planning to tell her about Paris—and why he'd gone there.

"And not just biscotti," he continued, "but—"

A commotion in the corridor cut short whatever he'd been about to say. In the next instant, Carl burst through the door. Dressed in a black hooded slicker, his face dripping with water, he reached his employer in a few loping strides. "Sir," he rasped, "Patches is loose!"

Holt slammed down his mug and rose from his chair. Andrea rose, too. "How did that happen?" he demanded.

"Well, sir . . ." Carl mopped his wet face with the back of his hand. "I'd gone into her stall to give her some fresh hay and she reared up." He gestured wildly. "The wind must've blown the barn door open, and when I backed off from the stall, she took off like the devil himself was after her. By the time I knew what was goin' on, she was out of there."

Holt brushed past Andrea as if she were invisible. "Let's go then, Carl. We have to find her." At the door, he suddenly turned back to Andrea. "If you'll excuse us, Miss Lane—"

Andrea watched for a second. "Wait!" She ran after him. "I'm going with you."

Holt swung around with such force that Andrea had to brace herself in the doorway to keep from losing her balance. "No. You're staying here."

Why should he be so upset with her? Surely he didn't think she was so fragile she couldn't weather a rainstorm. "Aren't three pairs of eyes better than two?" she challenged.

Holt's face came perilously close to hers. "You'll only get lost, and then we'll have the trouble of looking for you *and* Patches."

Andrea's temper flared. "So you think I'm not competent enough to find my way around? Well, Elizabeth's done such a good job of showing me the trails that I know them by heart."

"She's got a point," Carl interjected.

No one said anything for a tense moment. Then Holt took a step backward, allowing Andrea a fraction of space. "All right," he said, "come with us."

They trooped in silence down the hallway. At the kitchen, Holt made a detour, returning with two yellow-hooded slickers, two pairs of heavy gloves, and two sets of boots that looked as if they'd seen combat duty. "Here," he said, tossing Andrea the smaller of the two slickers.

It was obvious he was perturbed with her. It showed in his stiff stance, the tightening of his jaw when his fingers accidentally brushed hers in passing. Was he still unconvinced that she could take care of herself? She was tempted to tell him that he needn't fret. Nanna had taught her to hold her own in adverse circumstances.

Biting her tongue, Andrea pulled on the boots and shrugged into the slicker. She yanked the gloves over her hands and followed the men out.

The wind howled; the rain came in sheets from a sky almost as black as night. Andrea bowed her head and pushed sopping strands of hair away from her face. She found herself struggling to keep on the path that led to the barn.

The horses whinnied and pawed the floor restlessly as the two men saddled them. Rusty tossed his head, fighting the bit that Carl pushed into his mouth. Andrea took Shadow's reins and spoke gently to the mare.

There was a moment of quiet after the horses were saddled, when everyone seemed to grow calm. Holt passed a flashlight to Andrea, another to Carl, keeping a third for himself.

"Are we ready?" he said. "Carl..." He looked in the stable hand's direction. "Why don't you search along the Ivy Fork Trail. Miss Lane and I will take the Raven's Route and West Trail. Let's give ourselves an hour. Then we'll meet back here." He waited while they all checked their watches. "Even if one of us is lucky enough to find the pony, she might be caught in the brush or have tumbled into a hole. She's certain to be scared and difficult to handle. We may have to call for John's help."

Andrea saw that he spoke to Carl, ignoring her, and she ducked her head, looking away from him as they led the horses to the rear entrance of the barn.

"Miss Lane."

She turned slightly. Though his handsome face was concealed in shadow, the grim set of the full, generous mouth was clearly visible.

"What, Mr. Carraday?"

"We'll be in close proximity of each other most of the time. If you come across the pony, signal me with your light. Two flashes, then a pause and another flash."

She nodded, then put her back to him as she mounted Shadow. Part of her was glad at the knowledge that he wouldn't be far away from her in the darkness and the rain, while another part resented that he felt he must hover over her as if he were sure she would get lost.

They rode together along the Raven's Route until they reached the first intersection of the West Trail. "You take the West Trail," Holt directed her.

"No, I'll take the Raven's Route." Before he could argue the point, she spurred Shadow, and the mare took off at a healthy trot. Despite the weather and the circumstances,

Andrea felt a brief surge of satisfaction. Then she settled down to the serious business of looking for the pony.

Andrea slowed the mare and proceeded with caution along the trail. She gripped the reins with one hand, using the other hand to hold the flashlight aloft. Time after time, she swept the beam of light in an arc over the brush and bramble at the sides of the trail. The light reflected back the twisted shapes of dwarf pine and scrub oak trees and the thin wisps of fog that snaked around the slender branches like the fingers of some goblin out of a spooky fairy tale. The silence was eerie, but Andrea was grateful for the meager protection the vegetation offered from the elements.

The clean smell of rain and the sharp odor of wet pine needles filled her nostrils. But a chill crept past the shell of the slicker and the two sweaters she wore, and her arm began to ache from swinging the flashlight back and forth. Her cheeks stung from the slap of branches dashed into her face by the wind. Worse than the physical discomfort was her mounting sense of frustration.

With each sweep of the flashlight, she grew more anxious to locate Patches. She saw nothing except for the occasional beam of light slicing through the darkness from the West Trail, evidence that Holt was nearby. Once, the light shone directly on her, and she sent a brief signal back before continuing on.

The ache in her arm turned to numbness, and she lost most of the feeling in her fingers and hand. She slowed Shadow to a halt, dismounted and paced back and forth, flapping her arms in an effort to increase the flow of blood to her hand.

Some sound, a soft rustling in the brush, brought her to a stop. Guessing that it was Admiral, she trained her flashlight on the trail. There was no trace of the white horse and its rider. Disappointed, Andrea swung the light in a wider circle and peered into the brush. Another noise, like the snapping of a branch in two, cut the silence. She leveled the light in the direction of the noise.

A big brown eye, wide with fear, stared back at Andrea,

and she cried out in surprise. "Patches," she gasped as the pony's head came into view. The animal was caught in a thicket, just as Holt had surmised. Andrea reached into the tangled web of vines and branches, feeling her way until she made contact with the pony's nose. "There, there, Patches," she said. "It's all right. We'll get you out."

The pony snorted and tossed its head in response. Was the animal injured or just scared out of its wits?

Working quickly, Andrea marked the location of the thicket by spearing one of her gloves on a bare tree limb. Then she mounted Shadow and set off to find a place where the Raven's Route and West Trail converged.

The rain picked up, relentlessly slapping her cheeks with cold, wet drops and causing her to tremble as she flashed the agreed-upon signal in the direction of West Trail. Though she estimated the Raven's Route was no more than a mile or so in length, the going was slow, and her arms and hands soon grew numb again. The image of the pony's fearful eyes and its flaring nostrils was burned in her mind, and she urged Shadow on.

When she felt as if she could go no farther, she heard someone call her name. Peering around, she was disappointed to see nothing except rain dripping from the black trees. Was the wind playing tricks on her? Or her own mind?

"Over here, Miss Lane."

She knew with a certainty that the wind—or her own imagination—could never imitate the way he said her name. She reined Shadow in with such an abrupt jerk that the mare nearly stumbled. When the figure of Holt sitting astride Admiral emerged from the darkness, strange fairy-tale–like images spun through Andrea's head.

There are no brave knights, she reminded herself. But at that instant Holt Carraday resembled one, and it was a moment before she called out, "I've found Patches!"

The white horse came up alongside Shadow. Its rider's eyes met Andrea's. "Good work," Holt said, but his expression was hidden from her.

Andrea led him to the place where she'd impaled her glove on the branch. She directed her flashlight at the thicket.

Holt dismounted Admiral and peered into the brush.

"Can we get Patches out by ourselves?" Andrea asked anxiously.

"I wouldn't attempt it," Holt replied. He turned and looked at her for a long moment. "You're shivering."

"I'm fine."

He took off his glove and placed the palm of his hand against her cheek. "You're as cold as ice."

The unexpected intimacy of his touch, the incredible warmth of his skin next to hers, caused shivering of a different sort. The edge of his thumb moved over her cheek, grazing the scar. With a stifled cry, she pulled away. Her breath came in measured gasps until finally he spoke.

"I'm taking you back to the house. Now," he said gruffly. "You've got to get into some dry clothes."

Before she could argue with him, Holt got back on his horse and told her to do the same.

"But Patches..." she said.

"Patches isn't going anywhere, and your freezing to death won't be of help to her. Besides, Carl's probably returned to the barn. I'll need him to call for John's assistance."

As Holt had guessed, Carl was waiting for them at the stable. He looked wet and miserable, but his mood changed the moment Holt related the news about Patches. He even shot a grin Andrea's way and stuck his thumb in the air.

Over her protests, Holt insisted that Andrea stay mounted, and he rode beside her on his own horse to the rear door of the mansion. Laura met them with an anxious expression and a dozen questions, all of which Holt answered while at the same time instructing her to "see that Miss Lane gets a hot drink and a dry change of clothes." Pausing, he said, "How is Elizabeth?"

"She fell asleep, though she did ask for you, sir," Laura replied. "She asked for you, too." The housekeeper directed a smile at Andrea. "I told her you'd both gone on an errand,

and that we'd read for a little while together. After pouting a bit, she settled down."

A look of gratitude crossed Holt's face. "Thank you, Laura," he said, then turned to go.

Without thought, Andrea caught his arm, holding him back. Through chattering teeth, she managed to extract a promise from him that he would let her know immediately on his return about the pony's condition. After he left, Laura accompanied Andrea upstairs to her rooms and helped her out of her rain-soaked clothes and into a dry sweater and pair of slacks.

Andrea discovered that her hair was a mess, too, and Laura brought a towel from the bathroom. "Here, let me help," the housekeeper said. She blotted the wetness from Andrea's hair. "You have beautiful hair," she commented softly as she brushed the tangles out of the long strands.

Smiling, Andrea thanked Laura for the compliment. It wasn't until she'd gone into the bathroom and looked into the mirror that she realized Laura must have seen the scar. It stood out angrily against her pale cheek.

Closing her eyes, she remembered the touch of Holt's thumb on the roughened patch of skin. She swallowed the sob that rose in her throat and tried to calm her thoughts as she savagely applied a thick layer of concealer to her face.

A short time later, Andrea sat ensconced in one of the chairs by the fire in Holt's study. She'd come downstairs at Laura's insistence after the housekeeper assured her she would not only be warmer in the study, but that Mr. Carraday would want her to wait for him there.

Laura brought in a blanket, which she wrapped around Andrea's feet and legs. Sybil appeared next, bearing a tray filled with plates of sandwiches and fruit and a white teapot with matching cups.

Left alone, Andrea sipped at her tea and picked at a ham sandwich that seemed to have no taste. Around her, the ships in their glass cases shimmered in the light thrown from the fire, and for a moment Andrea imagined they were real ships on a sun-gilded sea. From some corner of her mind floated a snippet of a poem—and the rare memory of her father reading the poem to her from *A Child's Garden of Verses*.

> *" 'I should like to rise and go*
> *Where the golden apples grow;*
> *Where below another sky*
> *Parrot islands anchored lie,*
> *And, watched by cockatoos and goats,*
> *Lonely Crusoes building boats . . . ' "*

A tear tracked slowly down her cheek. She wiped it away and thought about her father, about Holt and his daughter, about herself, too, and the disparate ways people handled their grief.

She helped herself to another cup of tea and watched the fire until at last she heard footsteps. For an instant she thought there was a tapping sound as well, and she automatically tensed, preparing herself in case Jayne Evernham marched into the room. Her fears evaporated like mist at the first blaze of dawn when she saw the familiar figure of Holt standing in the doorway.

His slicker was gone, and he wore dry clothes. Only the damp hair that lay in glistening black curls at the base of his neck gave evidence that he'd been through a downpour.

He stood by the hearth for a few minutes, warming his hands. Then he sat down in the empty chair. "You look very comfortable there," he said with a glance in Andrea's direction.

"Patches . . ." she began.

"Is back in her stall, safe and dry and munching on her hay."

"Then she's all right?"

He sighed. "Except for a few scratches and a slight limp. I'll call the vet in the morning, have him come to check her for any serious injuries. But the consensus among John, Carl, and myself is that other than being badly frightened, Patches is none the worse for wear.''

Glimpsing Holt's face in profile, Andrea saw the weariness etched in his features. He did care deeply for his daughter. He did love her, as he'd said. "How did you manage to get Patches out of her predicament?" Andrea asked quietly.

He poured a cup of tea from the white pot and cradled it in his hands as he watched the fire. "John brought his pruning shears. After a lot of snipping, he was able to clear a path for us to reach the pony. I caught hold of her reins, and with some coaxing and cajoling, she walked out—under her own power, as the saying goes." He took a swallow from the cup. "But the real credit goes to you for finding her."

"It could as easily have been you or Carl."

He didn't reply, only reached for the plate of sandwiches and passed it to her. "I guess this is meant to substitute for dinner," he said.

This time, when she bit into her sandwich, she was able to taste the salty ham, the yeasty bread. The crisis with Patches was over, and she could relax. But when she heard the wind moan loudly, she suddenly tensed. The sound jarred a memory, and she recalled the one other time in her life when she had been so thoroughly chilled to the bone.

Frightful scenes from the past swirled uncontrollably through her mind—images from the frigid winter night when she'd been certain she would die at the hands of the man who'd held her at knife-point on a deserted Boston street, demanding her purse and her jewelry. She could see now his eyes livid with rage as he discovered all she had on her was ten dollars and an inexpensive watch.

"Lady," he'd shouted, his face a mask of hate, "you're gonna remember this night forever!" With horror, she saw again the blade of his knife gleaming in the moonlight as he raised it to her cheek.

Her hand came up to feel the scar; her other hand, shaking, almost dropped her cup of tea. Vaguely, she realized that Holt had risen, and she concentrated on steadying herself. After a minute she got up from her chair and carefully set her cup and plate on the tray.

"Will you tell Elizabeth about Patches?" she asked, seeking to maintain a calm voice.

"Of course," he said softly, "in the morning when we have breakfast together."

Andrea nodded and murmured an excuse that it was getting late. She dared to glance back. Holt stood watching her, and the forlorn look in his gaze made her think of lonely Crusoes building boats.

Was he really like that mythical man on an island—so out of touch with the world socially that he wanted the company of his daughter's tutor? Or had he noticed her sudden distraction and was puzzled over whether he had done something to cause it? Her heart ached to stay, and it was only with a gritty sense of resolve that she made herself walk away from Holt. Then all at once, her left foot snagged on some object, the blanket perhaps, and she went pitching forward.

At first she was conscious only of arms enfolding her, breaking her fall. Then she became aware of the scent of the woods mingled with the sea, and she found that her face was pressed against Holt's sweater and that he was pulling her closer. The rough fabric was all that separated her palms from his flesh as he tightened his hold on her.

She clutched at his sweater. His heart beat strong and steady against her cheek; his breath warmed her ear. An inner peace began to spread through her like the benevolent warmth of the sun on a summer's day, a sense of comfort that she'd never known in Alan's arms. She feared that she was dreaming and would soon waken to find herself in the canopied bed, her hands grasping at the cold sheets.

But it wasn't a dream, and slowly, Holt began to back away from her until all contact between them was broken. She couldn't bear to meet his eyes again as she muttered a clumsy apology. The words died on her lips when her gaze focused on the doorway and the shadowy figure of Jayne Evernham came into view. Despite the distance separating them, Andrea felt the woman's loathing for her.

"What's wrong?" Holt said. His voice sounded strained.

The expression of concern on his face almost convinced her that he had seen Jayne, too. But his attention was focused on her alone, and when she glanced at the doorway, Jayne was gone. "Not . . . nothing," she stammered.

"Good night then, Andrea," he said in a whisper.

She almost came to a halt. "Good night. . . ." Had he realized he'd called her by her first name?

Each step she took away from him was laced with dread—and a longing that shamed her. She couldn't say which was worse, the idea of facing a wrathful Jayne Evernham or the need to have Holt take her in his arms once more.

In the corridor she stopped and scanned its length for some sign of the old woman. The hallway was empty. Jayne had slipped away again, like a shadow in the night.

Chapter Eight

"Strawberry jam is my favorite. What's yours?"

"I'd have to say strawberry, too, though I'm also fond of peach." From the angle where she sat on the side of Elizabeth's bed, Andrea observed the girl as she ate a bite of her toast. Propped up against an array of pillows and flanked by Mrs. Muffin and Miss Violet, Elizabeth looked even more wan and fragile than usual. "Laura says that your fever's gone, so if you're up to getting out of bed later, I thought we could read together for a while or do a puzzle."

"Why can't I go see Patches?"

Andrea smoothed back a wisp of blond hair from the girl's forehead. "I don't know if that's a good idea."

"But I feel lots better now," Elizabeth protested.

Andrea rose and went over to the window. Sunlight streamed through the glass, and a surprisingly warm breeze rushed in when she opened the window a wide crack. She made a decision. "I think you're right. We should pay Patches a visit," she said, returning to the bed.

Elizabeth's eyes brightened. "Dad said she ran away, but you found her, and Dr. Carver told Dad that she must've hurt her leg on a briar so she has to stay in her stall."

"I'm sure it won't be very long until Patches's leg heals up."

"Maybe a week." Elizabeth picked a piece of strawberry from the jam and put it in her mouth. "Dad's gone away on business."

Andrea's stomach tightened at the news. "He left this morning?"

"Uh-huh. He went to Winnipeg," the girl said matter-of-factly. She laid her slice of toast on the tray that was in front of her.

Andrea made a pretext of straightening the soft down comforter and plumping the pillows behind Elizabeth's head. The night before she'd rested poorly, her sleep filled with jumbled images. Several times she'd sat up in bed with a start, her heart racing, knowing that she had dreamed of Holt and of the raven.

Once she'd gotten out of bed and gone to sit on the love seat. The rain had stopped and a silky seam of moonlight wove its way through the thin, high clouds. Sitting there in the dark, with only her thoughts for company, she'd heard a clamor coming from the corridor—Holt's voice, then Jayne's answering sharply. It was Jayne, wasn't it? Had Holt confronted his aunt about her conduct with Elizabeth? Or was it only Andrea's imagination that the other voice had been Jayne's? Shivering, she'd hurried back to bed and huddled under the covers.

"Miss."

Andrea dropped the pillow in her hands. "Sybil." She whirled around to face the cook.

"Sorry if I startled you." Sybil eyed her with a frown. "I just came to see if the child's done with her breakfast and ask if you want to eat yours in your room."

"In my room would be fine. Just some juice, toast, and tea, please."

The cook nodded, then turned to Elizabeth. "Laura will come shortly to see if you're up to a bath today." Without waiting for a response, she hustled out of the room.

Minutes later, Andrea stood in her shower, letting the hot water run over her shoulders and back. She thought of how wonderful and right it had felt to be in Holt's arms—and what an insane notion it was to want to be held by him again. His leaving had been opportune, she decided. She would have the chance to compose herself. When he came back, they would be on formal terms again.

And if we aren't? She pushed the question aside as she turned off the water and vigorously toweled herself dry.

"Looks like you survived in pretty good shape."

"What?" Andrea had been only half listening. She'd been too intent on watching Elizabeth grooming her pony in its stall. "Oh . . . yes." She glanced over at Carl, who stood with his right foot hitched on one of the bars of Rusty's stall. "I'm glad everything turned out okay."

"The kid's real attached to the pony, has been since the day her dad brought it home."

"Yes, I've noticed."

"Ya see, Miss Lane . . ." He lowered his voice to a confidential tone. "Mr. Carraday bought her the pony last year. Asked me to give her riding lessons. Appears he had the idea that taking care of the animal would, you know, bring her out of herself. The kid's been like that—shy, scared of her own shadow—ever since, well . . ." He reached in his shirt pocket and drew out a fat cigar. "Haven't smoked one of these in six months now. The doc said if I didn't quit, I'm apt to wind up dead in a few more years." He rolled the cigar between his stubby fingers, then shoved it back in his pocket. "I always carry one with me in case I change my mind."

It was amazing, thought Andrea. A few days ago she wouldn't have had this conversation with Carl. A few days ago she would've been fortunate if he gave her the hour of the day. "Do you think having the pony has helped her?"

"Yeah, sure." He patted the roan's rump. "Ya know, Mrs. Carraday couldn't abide horses, never set foot in the barn. Lots of things she couldn't abide, I reckon."

What things? Andrea longed to ask. The isolation of Ravenspire? Leaving an acting career to marry Holt Carraday? Enduring a loveless marriage? If what Maggie and Jayne said was true, then Holt had married Victoria out of passion. Had the beautiful Victoria ever loved him? Or had passion also driven her to accept his proposal? Or could it have been the promise of financial security?

Jayne had compared Victoria to Odette, the tragic heroine of *Swan Lake*. And she had compared Holt to the wicked von Rothbart. Had Holt treated Victoria badly? Andrea almost violently rejected the thought, though she couldn't rationally explain her feelings. But if Victoria had been distraught enough to take her own life, there had to be a good reason why.

Carl dragged his foot off the bar and faced Andrea. "You did a fine turn last evening, helping out. I figured you'd be like the rest of the teachers. Keep to yourself, never show your face around here." He took off his cap, twirled it in his hands, and set it on his head again. "I was wrong, Miss Lane."

She walked with him toward the front door of the barn. Just as he was about to go out, she said, "Thank you, Carl."

He tipped his cap to her and grinned.

Andrea moved back down the wide aisle, past the other stalls to the pony's. Stopping just outside the stall, she saw Elizabeth perched on a stool near Patches's right flank. The girl was brushing the pony's mane, chattering all the while to the animal. Andrea stood in the shadows for a moment, listening.

"I'll bring you a carrot to eat tomorrow," Elizabeth promised. "Then you'll get well, and I can take you out in the sunshine. Carrots are good for you, Dad always says. So are peas and squash. But I don't like squash."

Andrea smiled to herself. Squash was not her favorite vegetable, either.

"Dad never makes me eat squash." The girl sighed. "But once when he was away we had squash, and Auntie Jayne said I had to eat it. I told her my stomach hurt, but she made me eat every bite. Then I got sick and threw up, and Auntie Jayne yelled at me and said I wouldn't get any dinner for three nights and . . ."

Andrea gripped a bar of the stall. She must have said something aloud, though she had no recollection of what it was.

But Elizabeth came running toward her, arms outstretched. Andrea knelt down and embraced the girl.

"It's all right," she said. *Very soon,* she thought to herself, *very soon it will be. It must be.*

She held Elizabeth a moment, then she got up and helped the girl put away the stool and currying brush. They stopped once more at Patches's stall where Andrea fussed over the pony. The thought of going back to the house, of sitting down to eat her lunch in the dining room, held no appeal to Andrea.

"Elizabeth," she said, turning to the girl, "how would you like it if we ask Sybil to make us a picnic lunch and we ate outdoors?"

The picnic lunch proved to be a great success. Andrea purposely chose a spot under a gigantic fir tree in a corner of the yard that was hidden from the tower. There, she and Elizabeth spread their food on a large blanket and ate as they watched the puffy clouds floating through a china blue sky. Though Andrea worried that Elizabeth might get overly tired, she was pleased to notice the healthy blush of color that bloomed on the girl's cheeks.

After lunch they played catch for a while with a big red ball that Elizabeth had brought along. Then they packed the leftover food in the basket Sybil had provided and sat down on the blanket, their backs against the trunk of the tree, their legs stretched out in front of them.

A little burst of wind lifted a corner of the blanket, tearing at it. Andrea had to grab for the blanket and smooth it down. The incident brought back a certain memory.

"You know, Elizabeth, the way the wind blew the blanket reminds me of when Nanna and I went to a street fair."

"Who's Nanna?"

Andrea had to laugh at her slip of the tongue. "That's my grandmother. When I was very small, I couldn't pronounce the word grandma quite right, so since her name was Anna, I just called her Nanna. Anyway, every July, in the village where my grandmother lived in Oregon, the merchants hold a street fair. There's a Ferris wheel and a merry-go-round to ride on. And there are tents where they sell treats like fish and chips and ice-cream cones."

"And taffy? Dad buys me taffy when we go to Copalis Beach. I like the licorice flavor best."

Andrea tried to imagine Holt Carraday on a beach, buying his daughter taffy. "Yes, there was taffy, too. And there was a tent where they sold kites. Every summer Nanna would give me five dollars for the fair, and I'd spend it on rides and ice cream. But the year I was your age, I decided I'd rather spend my money on a kite. I found one that looked just like a gigantic butterfly with orange-and-yellow wings. It was the grandest kite I'd ever seen."

"I've never had a kite." Elizabeth sighed.

"No? We'll have to see what we can do about that. Anyway, I told Nanna that I wanted the kite, and she advised me that then I wouldn't have money left over for food or rides. I still bought the kite, and the next day I decided to test it out on the beach. Nanna warned me, 'Andy, the wind's too strong and that kite's a delicate thing.'"

"What's delicate mean?"

"Well, it can mean something that . . . isn't very strong, something that breaks easily." She glanced down at Elizabeth. "I didn't listen to Nanna. I flew my kite and thought to myself that it wasn't a delicate thing at all. Then a gust of wind came in off the water and carried the kite away. I tried to reel in the kite, but the wind took it even higher. I was looking up when suddenly I tripped over a chunk of driftwood. The next thing I knew, I was lying flat in the sand and the kite came crashing down beside me, all broken in pieces."

"Is that why you have a scar on your cheek?"

"What . . ."

"Did you get hurt when you fell over the driftwood?"

Andrea stared at the sky. "It happened another time."

The answer seemed to satisfy the girl. "Did you buy a new butterfly kite?" she asked, yawning.

"No, but I cried myself to sleep without dinner. The next

day when I came out to the kitchen for breakfast, there was my kite propped against the table, fixed good as new. Nanna had stayed up all night, mending the kite."

"I wish I had a Nanna."

So do I, thought Andrea. *I wish you had a Nanna instead of an Auntie Jayne. And I wish you had a mother and a butterfly kite.* She couldn't help wondering if Holt wished for those things, too, for his daughter.

"Tell another story about you and Nanna," Elizabeth pleaded, hiding a second yawn.

Andrea began the account of when she and Nanna went down to the dock with their fishing poles and ended up as extras on a movie set. But a glance at Elizabeth showed that the girl was fast asleep. Andrea realized that she felt drowsy, too. The afternoon had blessed them with its warmth; a breeze whispered like a lullaby through the fir tree. Closing her eyes, Andrea dozed off with images of butterfly kites and Nanna's soft, caring smile drifting through her mind.

Wakening to the trill of birdsong, Andrea felt momentarily confused. She rubbed her eyes and her vision cleared. Beside her, Elizabeth stretched her arms over her head. They smiled at each other, and Andrea noted that the shadows of the late-afternoon sun were beginning to lengthen over the grass. A coolness had crept into the air.

"I'm afraid our picnic's over," she said.

"Can we have another one tomorrow?"

"We'll see."

"If Dad's home, he can come with us."

Andrea rose from the blanket. Below the sun, the western sky was banked with heavy clouds. "It might rain this evening," she said.

Picking up the ball, Elizabeth bounced it against the tree trunk a few times, then with obvious reluctance put it away in the picnic basket.

After Andrea had shaken out the blanket, the girl helped her fold it into a neat square. They gathered up the basket and walked slowly back to the house.

* * *

It didn't rain that evening, at least not before midnight. The last Andrea checked the time it was ten to twelve, and light from the full moon shone through the windows, washing the carpet and bed in a sheen of silver.

Lying awake, she recounted the day she and Elizabeth had spent together. After they'd come in from their picnic, they'd read from *A Little Princess,* which Elizabeth had selected from one of the crammed bookshelves. Instead of going downstairs for dinner, they'd asked Laura to bring their meal to Andrea's rooms. They'd dined on their broiled salmon and roasted new potatoes while sitting cross-legged on the carpet in front of the love seat.

Afterward, Elizabeth had gone off with a certain air of secretiveness, only to return an hour later clutching a piece of paper in her fist. "I made this for you." She shyly handed the paper to Andrea.

It was a drawing of Patches with Andrea standing beside the pony. Touched, Andrea had thanked the girl and proudly hung the picture on the wall by the bureau.

If the evening had ended there, it would have been perfect, Andrea thought with chagrin. But she had decided to tote the tray of empty dishes back down to the kitchen instead of leaving them for Laura to pick up. On coming through the foyer, she'd realized too late that Jayne was standing in one of the dusky recesses like a cunning cat waiting for the hapless mouse to cross its path.

"Miss Lane." The old woman stepped from the shadows. "I'd like a word with you." Her long black skirt rustled as she moved forward and planted the cane in front of her toes.

Andrea berated herself for being weak-willed. She should have excused herself and walked away. But she'd stood there, holding the tray, and listened to Jayne railing against her for taking Elizabeth outdoors when she was ill.

"Victoria would never have allowed it," Jayne had declared. "The child's frail and should be protected, not exposed to the chill wind and damp ground."

How did you know we were outdoors? And how do you reconcile your idea that Elizabeth should be protected with your own cruel actions toward her? Andrea had bitten back the questions.

"She was such a loving mother," the old woman had said, her tone of voice low and reverent. Then she'd walked away, the cane rapping loudly with every step.

Andrea shivered, turned over in bed, and tucked one hand beneath her pillow. She had to shield her eyes from the moonlight that rippled across her bed. The vivid glow of moonbeams seemed surreal to her. Gloomy skies and driving rain lent a more appropriate backdrop to Ravenspire at night.

Shutting her eyes, Andrea envisioned another scene entirely. Ravenspire the way it was portrayed in the painting that hung in the foyer, its drab gray stones splashed with shades of lavender and rose. Though she tried to chase the image from her mind, she saw the brave knight charging from some far-off land to rescue the fair princess in distress. Drifting into sleep, she glimpsed beneath his silver helmet a cap of rough black curls and eyes the color of agates bathed in the cold, dark sea. She let out a soft cry. The knight was Holt, and on his shoulder sat the raven of her dreams.

A booming crack of thunder wakened Andrea. She sat bolt upright in bed, trembling and fully conscious. *Another nightmare,* she told herself. But she didn't recall dreaming of a storm.

After a moment, she threw off the covers, got out of bed, and padded over to the windows. There was no storm; not a cloud was visible in the night sky, only a dusting of stars and the moon shining lower through the trees.

Another sound like the tinkling of raindrops against glass drew her attention. It came from outside in the hall. Andrea's heart gave a loud slam as she got out of bed and crept over to the door. Cautiously, she opened the door a crack and peeked into the corridor. The hallway was empty, but she sensed something wasn't right.

Andrea hurried to the closet and put on her robe and slippers. Then she ventured into the corridor. Some object crunched under her foot. She looked down and saw what appeared to be a sliver of glass or china. All at once she realized what was wrong. The bust on the table was missing.

Not missing, she recognized with shock, but broken—smashed into dozens of pieces on the floor. The racket that wakened her must have been the statue toppling over.

Andrea began to creep along the corridor. Her gaze darted from one closed door to the next. When she came to Elizabeth's room, her breath caught in her throat. The girl's door was standing wide open.

"Elizabeth?" She strained to see in the yawning darkness of the room. There was no answer, so she went inside and switched on a lamp.

Elizabeth wasn't in her bed. The covers were tossed back and several of the fancy pillows were strewn about on the floor by the bed. A little knot of panic formed in Andrea's stomach. She sped into the corridor, calling the girl's name. Only silence greeted her. She tugged on each of the closed doors up and down the length of the hallway. All of them were locked.

Where could Elizabeth have gone to? Andrea asked herself as she descended the stairs. The passageway was nearly pitch black, and she had to feel her way with each step. At the bottom stair she saw a faint light coming from the foyer and, farther on, the corridor that led to the dining room and kitchen was illuminated. She walked past more locked rooms until she came to the kitchen door, which stood ajar.

After a second's hesitation, Andrea stepped into the kitchen. "Elizabeth!" she cried.

The girl was peering into the interior of an industrial-sized refrigerator. With her hands clasped around a milk carton, she looked for all the world like the proverbial kid who'd been caught pilfering from the cookie jar.

"What are you doing down here?" Andrea made a feeble attempt to hide her relief behind a stern exterior.

"I was thirsty," the girl said in a small voice.

A door at the other end of the long kitchen opened, and the cook poked her head around the corner. "What's going on?" she demanded.

Andrea made a dismissive gesture. "Nothing. Elizabeth wanted a glass of milk."

Sybil came shuffling into the kitchen. Her hair was askew, and she wore a voluminous, high-necked nightgown, which she clutched to her as if she feared some patch of flesh might accidentally show. She took the milk carton from Elizabeth's hands and fetched a glass from a row of tall cabinets that ran the length of one wall. "There." She poured milk into the glass and handed it to Elizabeth. "Now back to bed."

The girl darted a glance at Andrea, then the cook. "Thanks," she said, and ducked out of the kitchen.

Sybil got two more glasses from the cupboard and filled them with milk. "You look like you could use some nourishment, too." She plunked the glasses on a huge butcher-style table that ran along another wall of the room. Copper and stainless-steel pots and pans hung from numerous hooks above the counters. The kitchen appeared to have been designed with the idea of feeding a small army.

Andrea slumped into a chair across the table from Sybil. "I'm sorry we disturbed you."

"Never mind," Sybil said.

Andrea took a sip of milk—and made a decision to confide in Sybil. "Actually, I was asleep when a noise woke me. At first I thought it was a crash of thunder, but then I saw that it wasn't storming. So I went into the hallway to investigate further." She hesitated; Sybil leaned forward expectantly. "There's a statue," she continued, "that stands on a table in the corridor outside my room. I found it smashed to pieces on the floor, and then I realized that was what had wakened me."

The cook gave a loud gasp. "Don't tell me it's happening again!" she exclaimed.

"What's happening?" Andrea asked with alarm.

"The sleepwalking."

"Sleepwalking?"

Sybil batted at a stray wisp of hair with the back of her hand. "No reason you should have been told, Miss, but the sweet child's had problems ever since her mother . . . passed away. The sleepwalking started directly after Mrs. Carraday's death. The first time it happened, Laura found the child in the Grand Hall, curled in a knot, her thumb stuck in her mouth. Curious thing. We never found her in the Hall again, though she wandered off to plenty of other places. She'd have gone outside, if we hadn't locked the doors at night."

The cook gulped a swallow of milk. "Once I came into the kitchen and got the scare of my life. Here sat the child in the middle of the floor with broken glass all around her. She'd knocked over some fancy stemware that I'd left settin' out. Poor imp, could've been cut to ribbons if I hadn't snatched her up."

A chill seized Andrea. "Then you think Elizabeth was sleepwalking and pushed the statue onto the floor?"

"Must've been," the cook said with a shrug. "Don't worry, Miss. The child won't get in trouble for it. I'll tell Laura first thing when she comes in. I expect she'll pass the news on to Mr. Carraday. Heaven knows the man's tried," she added, scratching her head.

It was the first time Andrea had heard anyone at Ravenspire express outright sympathy for Holt Carraday. She was surprised that it had come from the cook.

Sybil polished off her milk. "Best that I get back to bed, Miss. "It's five A.M. by my watch, and everyone'll be expecting their breakfast in a couple more hours."

Andrea sat in the kitchen alone, nursing her glass of milk, more dubious than she wanted to admit about Sybil's explanation of the statue's demise. On the surface, the cook's reasoning sounded logical, and she had to believe Sybil was telling the truth about Elizabeth's sleepwalking. That revelation in itself was deeply troubling to Andrea. But the statue was fairly bulky and not light in weight.

How could a child of Elizabeth's size, while fast asleep,

have knocked over the statue with such force that it broke into scattered pieces? Wouldn't the commotion have wakened her? And if so, wouldn't she have been confused and frightened? The girl's actions—tramping down to the kitchen for milk—didn't denote fear. Her only comment had been that she was thirsty.

A disturbing suspicion took root in Andrea's mind. She reasoned that a good sturdy cane in capable hands could prove to be a fair weapon in the right circumstances. Jayne Evernham certainly had the strength to send a clay statue sailing to the floor. But what was her motive? To frighten the new tutor?

Or maybe Holt has talked to her, thought Andrea, *and she knows her days here are numbered and is now out for revenge.*

If Jayne had committed the deed, how she had managed to disappear completely undetected baffled Andrea, since all the doors in the upper hallway were locked—except for Elizabeth's, perhaps. Had Jayne slipped into the girl's room, as she did on those nights when she told Elizabeth stories? Or she might have keys to various rooms of the mansion. That could explain how she pulled off her vanishing act at the times Andrea had caught her spying.

Andrea rose from the table, leaving behind her nearly untouched glass of milk. She paced down the corridor, casting a nervous glance over her shoulder every few seconds. She saw only her own shadow and heard only her own footsteps. No doubt Jayne Evernham was safely back in her lair, gloating over her mischief.

Or, Andrea wondered, *am I just going crazy from listening to Jayne's rantings every night?*

Chapter Nine

Andrea had barely gotten back into bed when it was time to get up for the day. She crawled out from under the cozy covers and hurriedly dressed in a navy-and-white checked skirt and matching navy sweater.

Entering the corridor, she saw that the floor beneath the table was swept clean. Undoubtedly, Laura had taken care of the broken statue with her usual efficiency. Andrea's gaze lingered for a moment on the bare table, then she moved on. At each door she passed, she couldn't stop herself from putting her hand on the knob and twisting it to see if the door would yield. None of them did. She paused at Elizabeth's door, ready to knock, then changed her mind and went on down the stairs.

Elizabeth's chair in the dining room was empty, and there was no place setting laid out for her on the table. Disappointed, Andrea ate alone. She thought Sybil might make some reference to their earlier conversation about Elizabeth, but all the cook offered was an abrupt, "Will that do for now, Miss?" as she delivered breakfast.

No one else was about until Laura hurried into the room and began to rummage through a drawer in the sideboard. Andrea saw her opportunity.

"Laura?"

The housekeeper turned around. "Hi, Andrea," she said.

"Do you know if Elizabeth's sleeping in this morning?"

Laura laughed softly. "She never sleeps in, unless she's sick. She was here, wolfing down her breakfast half an hour ago. I believe she's gone to see her pony."

"I'll find her at the barn then."

The housekeeper gathered up what appeared to be a folded tablecloth and started across the room with it. "Mr. Carraday called this morning, said he'd be in late this afternoon or evening. I thought you'd like to know."

Andrea smiled a quick, nervous smile. "Yes, thank you."

"All right. Have a nice day," Laura called as she disappeared out the door.

Andrea stared after the housekeeper. If there'd been a crisis in the night, one would never guess it from Laura's behavior. As always, Laura had been congenial. She smiled easily. Yet there was something about the young woman that gave Andrea the impression she measured her every word, weighed her every gesture, so that she gave no one cause for offense.

Andrea sighed. She liked Laura a lot, but she was coming to realize that Laura was not apt to talk openly about something she viewed as a confidential matter.

After finishing her breakfast, Andrea wandered down to the barn. She found Elizabeth in Patches's stall, talking to the pony. The girl must have sensed that someone was approaching, for she suddenly grew quiet. But when Andrea stepped into the stall, Elizabeth looked excited to see her. She looked rested and alert, too, not like a child who had spent a good part of her night roaming the corridors of Ravenspire in her sleep, sending clay statues to their doom.

They lavished considerable attention on Patches. Andrea helped Elizabeth curry the pony, and she was happy that its leg appeared to be healing nicely. Once, Carl came into the barn. He waved and smiled at Andrea as he took Rusty from his stall. Then, whistling a snappy tune, Carl saddled up the gelding and rode off.

On the way back to the house, Elizabeth led Andrea on a detour around the garage. A jumble of large wire cages on wooden stilts leaned precariously against the stone wall.

"We used to have lots of rabbits," Elizabeth said. Her fingers curled around the wire of one of the cages. "Dad raised them for a hobby, but I liked to play with them, especially Sylvester. He was cuddly, a brown-and-white angora with big floppy ears.''

The revelation surprised Andrea. She tried to visualize the cages filled with rabbits and Holt working with them. Did he think Sylvester was cuddly? Did he lose his usual cool reserve when he was around his rabbits and talk to them and pet them? ''Why did your father get rid of the rabbits, Elizabeth?''

''He said he didn't have the proper time to devote to them, so he sold them all.'' The girl gazed up anxiously. ''Could you ask him to buy another rabbit? I know Dad'll get one if you ask him.''

Andrea looked away. Why would Elizabeth believe her father would buy a rabbit for the new tutor? ''We'll see, Elizabeth. Now . . .'' She put her arm around the girl. ''Let's get back to the house. It's almost noon.''

After lunch, they spent most of the afternoon in Elizabeth's rooms. Elizabeth watched a video about songbirds while Andrea pored over the lesson plans and tutorial guides and catalogs that she found in the drawers of the large desk.

Andrea made a list from the catalogs of materials that she deemed necessary, including art supplies for Elizabeth. She doubted that Holt would object if she splurged a bit on paints and brushes and an easel for his daughter.

An uncomfortable feeling of warmth spread through Andrea at the thought of seeing Holt again. She tried to picture their meeting when she approached him with her list of supplies. They would greet each other politely. He would ask what she needed; she would show him the list. He would give his approval in a cool, businesslike tone. Their conversation would be finished. She would go up to her rooms; he would resume whatever activity he was engaged in when she interrupted him.

Everything would be as it was before he held her in his arms. *It can never be the same,* her heart cried. *It must be,* the voice of reason answered. The embrace they'd shared meant nothing to him. She had tripped; he'd done the gentlemanly thing and caught her. Then why had he gathered her to himself, much closer, tighter than necessary, if he'd merely meant to keep her from falling? Abruptly, Andrea rose from the desk and looked out the curtainless windows.

Elizabeth came to stand beside her, and the two of them stared at the view of sky and tress until Andrea made the excuse of needing to change her clothes for dinner.

A few minutes later, Andrea stood in front of her closet, surveying her wardrobe. She couldn't decide what to wear. Every article of clothing she owned displeased her in some way. The peach crepe dress with its flowing skirt was much too formal attire for the gloomy dining room. The blue-and-green paisley print looked splashy and loud. The plain black sheath was ... Andrea shuddered. She would never put on anything black as long as she lived under the same roof as Jayne Evernham. Finally, she decided on her beige wool dress with the cowl collar.

Just as she was taking out her jewelry box, a knock came at the door. Andrea turned. Her sleeve caught on a corner of the box. The box flipped over on the carpet, spilling its contents.

"Andrea? Are you there?"

"Come on in, Laura." Andrea scooped up the necklaces and pins that were scattered on the floor.

"I'm sorry to bother ... Oh, here, let me help." Laura retrieved a necklace and a couple of pins that Andrea had missed. She dropped them in the jewelry box. "I just wanted to let you know that John and I are going to town for pizza, and I've asked Elizabeth to come with us."

Andrea had mixed feelings. There was relief on the one hand that Elizabeth had a chance to escape the dinner table. On the other hand was a sense of dread at the idea of facing Jayne alone over the evening meal. "Have a good time, Laura," she said, mustering a smile for the housekeeper.

When she entered the corridor to go downstairs, her gaze was drawn, as usual, to every closed door. What lay behind them? Rooms filled with dust-covered furniture and buckling floors? Cobwebs and closed, musty drapes? Or trapdoors and secret passageways that wound between the decaying walls of the mansion?

Andrea laughed at herself. There were no secret passageways at Ravenspire, just her imagination running wild from reading too many mystery stories.

Even before she reached the dining room, Andrea heard the old woman talking. Her steps slowed.

The sudden sound of a man's voice brought Andrea up short. She stood poised on the threshold, her eyes drawn to the figure of Holt. He paused in midsentence and got up from his chair, looking every inch the executive in his gray pinstriped suit.

"Please, come join us," he said, moving to pull out Andrea's chair for her.

"Thank you," she said, conscious that Holt's hands rested on the back of the chair, very near her shoulders. She was aware, too, that Jayne was keenly observing her every move. Her wine and water goblets were both filled. She lifted the water glass to her lips and took a sip.

"I understand that you and my daughter had a picnic yesterday."

Though Holt's mouth was curved in a slight smile, there was a pale, drawn quality about his face that startled Andrea. Was it simple jet lag or worry over business matters that caused the sudden deepening of the fine lines around his eyes? Or had he heard the news about his daughter's sleepwalking and was upset over that?

"Yes, we had a picnic," she said.

Jayne cleared her throat. "Elizabeth's been ill," she said in a querulous tone. She lifted her head and thrust out her chin. "I spoke to Miss Lane about the dangers of exposing the child to damp ground and cold air. You should realize by now, Holt, that there are consequences to be paid for such foolish—"

"I'm certain," he broke in, "that Elizabeth wasn't harmed at all by the fresh air."

"That's true, Mrs. Evernham." Andrea was surprised by the calmness of her voice. Perhaps it was Holt's show of support—or the knowledge that he was going to oust Jayne from the mansion—that gave her the courage to add, "In fact, I think Elizabeth needs to get out more often."

A chilling silence fell over the room as Jayne shook out her napkin and placed it in her lap. Andrea wondered again if Jayne knew her days at Ravenspire were numbered. If so, that would account for the venomous look she sent her nephew's way. But if Holt noticed the vile glance, he gave no indication of it.

The door to the kitchen swung open, and Sybil burst in with plates of roasted chicken and grilled vegetables. She served the food with an officious air and then left.

Andrea watched from under lowered lids as Holt and Jayne picked up their forks. She followed suit, and the three of them ate in an atmosphere of heavy silence. All the while, Andrea felt the old woman's eyes tracking her critically.

There was a clatter of silverware. Andrea looked up and saw that Jayne's knife and fork were crossed over her empty plate.

The old woman stood and, with a sweep of her black dress, strode around the table to her nephew's chair. Her skeletal hand came to rest on his shoulder. "You don't look a bit well, Holt," she said in a fawning tone.

He stared straight ahead. "I'm fine, Aunt Jayne."

"You've been working much too hard," she went on, ignoring his response. "You must remember that you're pushing forty. Why don't you plan a little vacation for yourself—get away to a place where you can be alone." Her voice became low, persuasive. "Remember how you and Victoria honeymooned in Switzerland? She loved the Alps, didn't she, Holt? What was that charming little village where you leased a chalet? Why don't you go there?"

Holt grabbed his wineglass, drained the last drops of liquid from the bottom. His hand trembled as he set the goblet by his plate. "I don't need a vacation." He ground out the words.

Andrea had never seen him so visibly shaken by something his aunt had said. Was it the mention of his honeymoon? Perhaps the marriage had been in trouble from the very first and Holt's passion had died in those first weeks of his marriage to Victoria, with little left to bind them together except the vows they had taken. Or the honeymoon might have been wonderful, and now the memory of it was too painful for him to bear.

"Come now," Jayne admonished. "It shows in your face, Holt. The worry, the strain, the lack of sleep. But you needn't concern yourself about matters here. You've hired Miss Lane to look after your daughter—"

"Miss Lane," he interrupted, "is Elizabeth's tutor, not her baby-sitter."

"Oh well, it's all one and the same, isn't it?" Jayne sounded benevolent; her countenance looked scornful. An odd smile suddenly lit her face. "Think about it, Holt," she said, "and you'll see that I'm right about taking some time off and going away alone." She turned and marched out of the room, her cane rapping triumphantly with each step.

Andrea darted a glance at Holt; he didn't return it, didn't see the sympathy that was written on her face.

He stared after his aunt for some time, his face white, his mouth set in a thin line. With deliberate slowness, he folded his napkin and laid it beside his plate. "It won't be much longer," he said, raising his eyes. "I'm in the process of making other . . . arrangements for my aunt's care."

Andrea replied with a nod when what she really wanted to do was say, *"It's about time."*

Holt's features relaxed a little. "Actually, I am planning a small trip down along the coast." He toyed with the stem of his wineglass. "Elizabeth told me about a street fair your grandmother took you to where you bought a kite that looked like a butterfly. My daughter's convinced that she has to have a butterfly kite, too, and that she'll be able to find one at a shop on the beach."

And now you're in the hot seat until she gets one, Andrea thought with amusement.

"We both agreed the day wouldn't be complete unless you joined us," he said. "Would you?"

Andrea's heart hammered out of proportion to the simple request. "I . . . yes, I'd enjoy that." Holt appeared to be anticipating her next move. Should she excuse herself or wait for a cue from him?

Finally, he pulled back the sleeve of his jacket and checked his watch. "If you'll excuse me," he said, "I have some paperwork to take care of."

Andrea started to get up. In an instant, Holt was at her side, assisting her with her chair.

Even without the presence of Jayne Evernham, the atmosphere in the shadowy dining room crackled with tension. Though their hands never touched and there was not the slightest contact between Holt's fingers and hers, Andrea felt the warmth of his skin, the vital power he projected as surely as if he had taken her in his arms a second time. Their eyes met, and intuitively she knew that he, too, was remembering their embrace. She sensed that their relationship had moved in a new direction and that he was as fearful as she was of where it might lead them.

They left the next morning right after breakfast, as Holt had promised. The sun was shining and there wasn't a cloud to be seen in the sky as they headed out in the Lexus. Nonetheless, they had all dressed appropriately for the late-fall season in jeans and sweaters. They'd each brought a jacket, too, for the weather could be unpredictable at that time of year, mild and sunny in the morning, then by afternoon dark clouds and rain blowing in from the ocean.

Holt's leather jacket lay folded neatly on the console between the front passenger seats. The brown leather was faded and cracked, the elbows nearly worn through. Andrea couldn't help envisioning Holt in the jacket, his thick black hair skimming the patched collar. She wondered if the jacket had been a gift from Victoria. Had his wife enjoyed going on day trips along the coast? *"Lots of things she couldn't abide,"* Carl had said. Had the Pacific Ocean been one of them?

As it was, the trip had started off on a bit of an embarrassing note for Andrea when Elizabeth scrambled into the backseat, and Andrea had been left with no choice but to take the front passenger seat next to Holt. If he had been uneasy with the arrangement, he'd given no indication. His manner had been pleasant, almost smiling as he turned toward his daughter and admonished her to buckle up.

As soon as they were on the road, Holt put on a CD of light classical music. The three of them rode along in companionable silence, and Andrea found herself looking forward to the day ahead. She had slept surprisingly well the night before. But when she'd wakened, she'd felt eager and flighty, like a caged animal that was about to be set free. Glancing into the backseat, she noted that Elizabeth's face was pressed close to the window, though the only view at the moment was of winding blacktop and trees.

They headed south, through the thickly forested hills of the coastal range to the twin seaports of Hoquiam and Aberdeen that straddled busy Grays Harbor. At Hoquiam, Holt pulled off the highway and drove into town. He found a parking place in front of a quaint-looking gift shop called The Sandpiper where colorful lanterns and fishing gear were displayed in the big bay window.

"You've been to Grays Harbor before?" he asked.

"No, never," Andrea told him. "My grandmother had cataracts, and she gave up driving when I was nine years old." It hadn't seemed like a hardship at the time, staying at Nanna's cozy cottage all summer, with the ocean just yards from the back door.

"Why don't we get out and watch the fishing boats for a while," Holt suggested.

They chose a wooden bench near a weathered-looking pier where boats with names such as *Sea Nymph* and *The Dolly Mae* were tethered. The boats bobbing on the water, the brisk, briny scent of the air, the men waving and calling to one another as they boarded their vessels, wakened memories in Andrea of the times she and Nanna would take a portable breakfast with them to the dock so that they could watch the fishing fleet go out.

A half dozen seagulls sat in a disorganized row on the pilings of the pier, crying for handouts from the men on the boats. With a great flapping of wings, the gray birds took flight, circling and diving over the decks until one of the men took pity and tossed something, perhaps brine shrimp, from a bucket into the water for the hungry hoard.

The colorful, cozy harbor, bustling with activity, seemed worlds away to Andrea from the foreboding isolation of Ravenspire. But when a man in a yellow knit cap on the *Sea Nymph* waved to them and grinned, Andrea imagined. *He thinks we're a family, husband and wife deeply devoted to each other and to their daughter, and all three happy and without a single care in the world because they are on vacation.*

Her eyes stung with sudden tears, and she looked away. A freighter was visible near the horizon. The huge ship was so far out that it appeared not to be moving.

It's an illusion, thought Andrea, blinking back the wetness in her eyes. Like the mistaken idea that she, Holt, and Elizabeth were a family. Or her long-ago dream of marrying Alan and having his children.

"Miss Lane, look." There was a tug on her sleeve.

"Yes, Elizabeth?"

The girl pointed at a seagull that was standing a few feet from the bench. It regarded them with unblinking eyes, a fish caught firmly in its beak.

"He's having his breakfast," Elizabeth said.

Andrea put on a bright smile and nodded. Glancing over Elizabeth's head, she saw that Holt was staring at her.

From time to time, Elizabeth got up from the bench to skip about or run the length of the pier and back. The girl looked as free as the gulls that wheeled and shrieked above her. But always, Andrea noticed, Holt kept his daughter in sight, and if she began to wander too far from the bench he would call her back or go and take her by the hand. After a while, he bought hot chocolate for Elizabeth and coffee for himself and Andrea from a dockside café.

When they were settled back down on the bench, he turned to his daughter. "Watch *The Dolly Mae*," he said. "They're getting ready to hoist the anchor."

On the boat, a man with bushy brown hair and a beard was reeling in a coil of wire that was attached to a pully.

Andrea stole a glance at Holt. In profile, he appeared at ease, with the wind ruffling his hair, his expression animated as he watched the men on the boat.

Suddenly, as if he knew she were observing him, Holt turned and met her gaze. His mouth curved in a full smile, and Andrea realized that she had never seen him look so at peace with his surroundings.

Andrea allowed herself the indulgence of watching him without restraint, of basking in the glow of his attention. Like a miser hoarding gold, she stored away the precious memory of his face as it looked in full sunlight, the expressive mouth with its flawless white teeth, the eyes that today reflected the dazzling blue of the sky. She wanted to tumble into those blue depths and uncover their secrets. She wanted to feel again the comfort of being held in his arms. She wanted to bury her fingers in the rough curls of his hair, to console him and submit herself to the charm of his kisses. She wanted—

"Dad?"

Andrea stifled a gasp. She blinked, tore her gaze from Holt. She stared at the pier, her mind dull and groggy, as if she'd been wakened from a beautiful and impossible dream.

A dangerous dream, she told herself. Dangerous to think that he could want her, need her. Besides, she barely knew him. But her heart was obviously bent on overriding all rational thought when it came to Holt Carraday.

"What is it, Elizabeth?"

Holt's voice was unnaturally thick, his words slightly slurred, and it seemed to Andrea that he spoke from a distance, as if he, too, were being roused from a dream.

"Can we go to lunch soon?"

He cleared his throat. "It's a bit early for lunch," he said, his voice almost normal again. "If you can wait another hour, I have a special place in mind for us to eat."

He got up from the bench, and his daughter jumped up to join him. Stiffly, Andrea rose. While Elizabeth skipped on ahead, she and Holt walked to the car without looking at each other.

They headed south once more, through the emerald green hills. Crossing the Naselle River, Andrea saw puffy clouds mirrored in the placid waters of Shoalwater Bay. Where the highway ended at Seaview, Holt turned the Lexus north onto Washington's Long Beach Peninsula. The wooded landscape gave way to flat marshes and cranberry bogs and quaint fishing villages that dozed in the noonday sun.

They drove as far as Nahcotta, creeping at a snail's pace behind a line of traffic through the village. At last, Holt pulled up beside a one-story cottage that appeared as if it had been left to its own devices for years. The white siding was peeling and faded purple shutters flanked the windows. But the tiny parking lot was jammed with cars, and a gaily painted sign that hung above the door read *The Oystercatcher.*

"It's not much to look at," Holt said, "but I think you'll be pleasantly surprised when you taste the food."

They were the first words any of them had spoken in miles except for a wistful question from Elizabeth about whether there was a shop on the peninsula that sold kites.

Andrea soon discovered that Holt's comment about the food was conspicuously modest. The Oystercatcher's specialty was, not surprisingly, oyster stew. It was the best Andrea had ever tasted. She and Holt consumed huge bowls of the thick stew, while Elizabeth ate a child-size portion of fish and chips.

Afterward, they strolled in and out of the gift shops that dotted the tiny village, working off their lunch and scouting for a place that sold kites. Andrea was too conscious of Holt's nearness as they gazed at paintings of the ocean in an art gallery. In another shop, when they were examining a wood carving of a lighthouse, Holt's hand accidentally brushed against hers as he explained some detail on the model, and a lump rose in her throat at the touch of his fingers on her skin.

It wasn't until they went to Ocean Park on the other side of the thin strip of land that they found a store that sold kites. The Rose Agate carried all manner of kites for all manner of tastes, from traditional to the bizarre. There were parachute kites, box kites, fighter kites, wind-sock kites. One kite was the spitting image of the *Voyager* spaceship, another of Mickey Mouse. But of all the kites on display, none resembled a huge orange-and-yellow butterfly. Finally, Elizabeth settled on a parachute kite that looked like a giant seagull.

Walking the hundred yards or so from the shop to the beach, Holt confessed with a smile, "I haven't flown one of these since I was ten years old."

Andrea tried to envision that child of ten, carefree and happy, having no other worries except whether his kite would catch the wind. The way he was studying her led her to believe that he was trying to imagine the same about her. "I haven't flown one since I was eight," she said, smiling, "but I doubt that either of us has forgotten how."

They both were a bit rusty, but in their joint effort they managed to launch the kite, and soon the Gull, as Elizabeth named the kite, was riding the wind high above them.

"Here, try it, Elizabeth." Andrea showed her how to control the kite string with one hand while holding the spool in the other.

"What if it falls?" Elizabeth's brow furrowed with uncertainty.

"It won't," Andrea assured her. "Your father and I will

make sure that it doesn't." Over Elizabeth's head, Holt smiled at her.

They flew the Gull, running up and down the beach, laughing and shouting warnings to one another whenever the kite appeared to be in danger of tumbling to the ground.

At last, Elizabeth tired of the game of kite-flying. While Andrea was helping the girl reel in the Gull, Holt announced that he had one more place he wanted to take them before they headed for home.

The place turned out to be Cape Disappointment Lighthouse, which was located on a rugged and breathtakingly beautiful slip of land at the southern end of the peninsula where the ocean met the wide mouth of the Columbia River.

"My great-grandfather's clipper ship, the *Raven,* came within a sail's breadth of sinking a couple of miles offshore," Holt said, pointing to a line of dark rocks jutting above the water. "That was before the lighthouse was built."

Andrea gazed down from the promontory where she and Holt stood. They had a clear view of the ocean, as well as the small empty beach below them where Elizabeth was hunting for agates.

"The *Raven*?" she echoed, glancing at Holt. He stood with his hands stuffed in his jeans pockets, wearing the leather jacket. Standing tall and straight, his legs planted apart, his face turned toward the water, Holt looked like a man renewed, invigorated with power. But appearances could be deceptive, Andrea knew, and his relaxed demeanor was apt to quickly change back into one of distraction the moment he set foot in his mansion.

"He'd sailed up the coast from San Francisco," Holt went on, "to survey the parcel of land he'd bought for the purpose of building a summer home."

"Ravenspire," she guessed.

"You probably noticed the carvings on the front door."

"They're carvings of your great-grandfather's ship?"

Holt nodded. "His name was Samuel Channing—Channing was my mother's maiden name. He was the one who started the family pharmaceutical empire." The comment was laced with a hint of sarcasm.

"So your company is based in San Francisco?"

"There and Vancouver." He glanced at her. "Sam Channing started out as a purveyor of homeopathic remedies. Tonics were all the rage in England and Europe at that time. My great-grandfather became friends with a well-respected and astute English physician who had developed a line of the natural remedies, and he contracted with the doctor to introduce them in America. Channing Pharmaceuticals was born in a storefront in New York City. In time, Sam Channing came west. He settled in San Francisco and expanded the business to include more conventional medicines."

"Was he married then?"

Holt drew his hands from his pockets and crossed his arms over his chest. "No. He met his future wife in San Francisco. After they married and my grandfather was born, Sam moved his family to the new estate—Ravenspire. His wife and son lived there year-round, while Sam spent a good part of his time in San Francisco running the business. Of course, the pharmaceutical empire was passed on to succeeding generations."

"Was your father involved in the business?"

"My father," Holt said bitterly, "was an opportunist who saw a way to financial nirvana by marrying my mother. Then he met the daughter of a shipping magnate. He dumped my mother to marry the shipping heiress. What about your family?" He turned to face her. "You said you had no one in Boston."

The veiled hurt in his eyes gave Andrea the courage to tell him the truth about her own father. "I was an only child, and after my mother died, my father . . . fell apart." She looked out over the view. On the far horizon, there was a thin but unmistakable edge of dark clouds. "He was an alcoholic. He quit drinking after he married my mother—and began again the week she died. He went through detox, tried AA . . ." She swallowed to ease the tightness in her throat.

"I realize now that he drank for the same reason that I buried myself in books. To escape the unbearable pain. A few years ago, he lost his job. Then he married a woman half his age and moved with her to North Carolina where her family lives. I haven't heard from him in over a year. I don't know if I ever will."

"I'm sorry."

Those two whispered words drew her gaze back to Holt. He held his arms rigidly at his sides, his hands curled into fists. His eyes telegraphed exquisite sympathy as they met hers. He said, "It's time we were heading home," but he didn't move, and they stood within inches of each other, their eyes locked in silent communion until Elizabeth called up to them from the beach.

Holt turned away then and took the lead on the path that wound down to the beach.

Elizabeth ran up to them, proudly displaying a piece of driftwood that she had found on the beach. "Can you carve a model of the *Raven* from it?" she asked her father.

He examined the piece. "The wood may be too soft," he said, "but I'll see what I can do."

Andrea stood by, a forced smile on her face, feeling on the verge of tears. She had spoken about her father's problems openly for the first time in years. And with his eyes and the simple words "I'm sorry," Holt had shown her that he understood.

They left Cape Disappointment, heading north along the same route they had come. The clouds that had been visible far out at sea crept inland, and by the time Holt pulled up beside a fast-food restaurant for hamburgers and milk shakes, the threat of rain was imminent. They made one other stop, in Aberdeen, where Holt dodged a smattering of raindrops to buy two boxes of saltwater taffy at a store—one for his daughter, the other for Andrea.

As they approached Seacliff, the moods of the three passengers began to match the gloomy cast of the sky overhead.

Their magical day at the coast was over, and they were going home to Ravenspire.

Holt slowed the Lexus at the sign and the statue of the raven. He swung into the driveway. The car passed under the arch of twisted tree limbs and emerged near the front of the mansion. Then something amazing happened. The sun broke through the thick blanket of clouds. Andrea's gaze was drawn to the house. "Wait!" she cried.

The Lexus jolted to a stop. "What's wrong?" Holt asked in a startled voice.

"Ravenspire," she murmured. "Look . . . the colors." In the fading light of the sun, the somber gray stones came alive with varying shades of rose and lavender. "The house looks just the way it does in your mother's painting."

"She's right, Dad," Elizabeth said from the backseat. "The house looks exactly the same."

He was silent a moment. "It's remarkable," he said at last.

Andrea glanced at Holt and saw something even more remarkable—the mansion, bathed in pastel hues, reflected in his eyes. Hope flared briefly in her heart, and she wished it wasn't foolish to believe in fairy tales.

Chapter Ten

"Don't you think it's odd, Miss Lane, that a man whose wife drowned would harbor such a fascination for the sea?"

Andrea chewed her bite of roast thoroughly before answering. "I think that each person has his own way of coping with the death of..." She almost slipped and said "a loved one." "... the death of someone they've held dear. So no, I don't find it unusual that... Mr. Carraday would still enjoy the water. Or that he takes pleasure in the hobby of miniature shipbuilding."

"Of course, Holt's ships—his darlings." The old woman regarded Andrea with a reproachful gaze. "Curious that Holt always manages to be gone each year on the anniversary of Victoria's passing. Victoria died on the twenty-first. Today is the seventeenth."

Was that why Andrea had found a note from him under her door when she'd wakened that morning? *I'll be away until the 22nd,* the note read in his bold writing. *I apologize that we haven't had the opportunity to talk further about my daughter.* He'd signed it *H. C.* Andrea had reread the note twice, then put it away in a drawer.

In the two days since their trip down the coast, she'd seen Holt only in passing. Their conversation had been reduced to mundane comments about the weather while their glances connected briefly, as if they were engaged in a formal waltz where neither party could quite look at the other and where both were determined to focus their sight on some invisible place that would keep them from stumbling over each other's toes.

It seemed more like a dream than reality that, for a few shining hours, she and Holt had let down their guards, had laughed and talked and flown a kite on the beach. She remembered how at ease he'd looked, with the sunlight reflected in his eyes and the wind blowing through the dense curls of his hair.

Now, if it wasn't for the box of taffy sitting on her bureau and the seagull kite propped in a corner of Elizabeth's room, she might have been able to convince herself that their day at the beach had never happened.

"The locals have a name for the cliffs where she fell," Jayne said, her voice lower, almost intimate. "They call them the Rocks of Destruction." She emphasized each syllable. "You might want to visit them sometime, Miss Lane. All you need do is follow the Raven's Route to where it ends at the footpath. The path will take you to the stone stairs."

The ones you told Elizabeth the Indians built to carry people to their deaths, thought Andrea.

Jayne folded her hands together. "I hear you've taken to Shadow. She was my horse, you know."

"She's very gentle—easy to handle." *Not at all like her former mistress.*

"She'll serve you well, I'm sure." The old woman's mouth twitched in a smile. "Now where was I? Oh, yes. If you climb the stone steps, you'll be there on the ledge, looking down at the very spot where Victoria fell. The rocks are quite jagged below, just their tips visible above the water." Jayne's eyes lit with a strange glow of excitement. "Victoria's body didn't wash up there, but the currents carried her farther north to a tiny beachhead. Otherwise, the waves would have dashed her to bits against the stone."

Shuddering inwardly, Andrea envisioned the beautiful Victoria, her body ghostly white and swollen from the salt water, deposited by the unforgiving sea onto the patch of beach. There was seaweed tangled through her blond hair—Andrea imagined that Victoria's hair had been very long and sleek—

and her lovely face bruised purple from the battering of the waves.

"There's another way up the rocks, on the opposite side," Jayne pushed on, "but it's a treacherous little path, and I wouldn't recommend that you follow it, Miss Lane, unless you're an experienced climber."

The candle flames wavered and sputtered as Andrea stared at them. She felt a sudden draft. *There must be a crack in one of the windowpanes,* she thought. She hardly noticed that Jayne had risen from her chair and come around the table.

Jayne rested her hand on the table near Andrea's plate. The veins bulged, blue and grotesque, under the sallow, crepey skin. "I'll bid you good night, Miss Lane," she said. There was the smell of wine and garlic on her breath. Andrea sat without moving until she heard the sound of the cane retreating down the corridor. Then she slumped back in her chair. She felt very tired.

The next afternoon, Andrea found an unexpected opportunity to visit the rocks. She'd spent the morning with Elizabeth at the barn, visiting Patches. Dr. Carver had come to check on the pony and pronounced her almost healed.

"Just a few more days," the kindly veterinarian had said with a wink and a smile in Elizabeth's direction, "and she'll be good as new again." On his advice, they had exercised the pony, walking her around the barn until it was time for the noon meal. After lunch, Elizabeth went to her rooms to watch *101 Dalmations*, which Laura and John had rented from the video store in Seacliff.

Seeing her chance, Andrea headed to the barn to saddle up Shadow. As she passed the tower, she was plagued by the thought that a pair of shrewd blue eyes was watching her progress from one of those lofty windows.

The sun shone brightly in the sky; the air was still and warm for late autumn as Andrea rode along the Raven's Route. When she reached the end of the trail, she tethered Shadow to a hemlock tree and started off down the footpath.

Weeds and twisted vines encroached on the path, making the way difficult. Andrea had to choose her steps carefully. After a quarter of a mile or so, the path opened out onto a clearing. Straight ahead was the set of stone stairs.

Mounting the stairs, she heard the murmur of the ocean, low and indistinct, like the hush of voices in a sickroom on learning the patient's condition is terminal. She caught her breath when her nose detected the fetid smell of rotting seaweed. Looking down, she got her first glimpse of the water through the bushes that grew alongside the stairs.

The climb was steep. Andrea's heart pounded in her ears by the time she came to a sharp curve in the stairs. She paused to rest and saw the Pacific spread out to the horizon. Sunlight rippled across the water, giving it the appearance of polished glass. The ocean looked calm; there was no wind. Pushing on, Andrea finally emerged onto the ledge that formed the top of the Rocks of Destruction.

Andrea gazed around her. The ledge was wide and flat in some places, making for easy passage, but dangerously narrow in others. She began to wend her way across the ledge toward a spot that would give her a full view of the ocean. She stopped when she saw that she wasn't alone.

A man stood not far from her, on the crag of a small promontory that jutted high above the water. Observing him for a moment, Andrea was struck by his appearance. Dressed all in white from his sweater to his slacks, with long silvery hair that fell straight to his shoulders, the man looked more angelic than mortal. She took a step forward, and the man turned toward her.

Staring into his face, Andrea decided that he was definitely earthly in nature, though with his distinct features ravaged by time—and who knew what else—he might qualify as an aging Apollo. Deep lines radiated from surprisingly sharp green eyes to form a busy network of creases over the sunken cheeks and high brow. There was an air about him that made Andrea wonder if he were an artist or a photographer by trade. Or maybe he was a writer. Many coastal villages along the moody Pacific were havens for thriving artists' and writers' colonies.

In any case, if he lived in the area, he was undoubtedly aware of the tragic history that overshadowed the spot where he stood. That meant he was apt to have his own opinions on the matter of Victoria Carraday's death. The possibility tempted Andrea. She resolved to attempt to engage him in a bit of conversation, despite the fact he was regarding her with an expression that was a mixture of curiosity and disdain.

Moving a little away from him, she peered over the cliff. There was a sheer drop from the crag to the sea far below. A shiver passed through Andrea when she spotted the rocks Jayne had spoken about. Their black peaks poked menacingly above the surface of the water. Farther out, huge seastacks soared skyward; here and there a stubborn tree clung to the tall fingers of stone, bowed and frazzled by the wind that continually raked through its branches. But today, the trees were still, and the rocks glistened in the sunlight.

"The ocean is beautiful, isn't it? Really spectacular," she said as an opening gambit. From the corner of her eye, she observed that the man had walked over to join her. She moved a bit closer to the edge to get a better view of the water.

"Watch out!" the man suddenly cried.

Andrea swung around in surprise. The man looked shaken, his face white as a sheet.

"Don't you know the rocks can be very slippery?" he said in a scolding—and very British—tone of voice. "One careless step and a young lady could lose her life."

His uncanny observation rattled Andrea. Inching away from the edge of the crag, she wondered if the man actually lived in the area, after all. "I understand it's common knowledge that a woman did lose her life in a fall from these very rocks," she ventured.

He cocked one slanted brow. "Oh?" he said.

"You're not from around here, are you?"

"You thought that I was?"

"I thought that you might be an artist. You're a tourist instead?"

"One and a half lucky guesses," he said with a disarming smile. "I'm an artist of sorts."

"The view of the ocean from here would make a beautiful subject for a painting."

"It would," he agreed, but without enthusiasm.

"Isn't this a bit off the beaten track for a tourist attraction, though?"

He crossed his arms over his chest. "I prefer off the beaten track. Is this a coincidence? Are you a tourist—and an artist—too?"

"Neither." Andrea looked away from him. "I recently moved to the area."

"You've aroused my curiosity, Miss..."

"Lane," she supplied.

"Tell me about the woman who lost her life here, Miss Lane."

She slid a glance his way. A faint breeze stirred the silver strands of his hair, lifting them away from his face, "I'll tell you what I know," she said. "Her name was Victoria Carraday. Maybe you've heard of her." There was no reaction on his part, so she continued. "Exactly what happened to Victoria that day a few years ago is a mystery. The sheriff ruled her death an accident, but rumor is that she took her own life because she was desperately unhappy."

"Ah!" the man said. "Intrigue. A local legend. But why was Victoria unhappy?"

Andrea hesitated, reluctant to drag Holt's name into the picture. "Apparently, she was having an affair with an actor—someone she'd been involved with before her marriage. Perhaps she wanted to be with him and knew that it was impossible. I can't tell you any more."

"I see. Well..." He pulled back his sleeve, exposing a wristwatch with a heavy gold band. "I'm loath to end such an enlightening conversation, Miss Lane, but I have a tour bus to catch. Be careful where you step," he cautioned, backing away from her. Then, with seeming disregard as to his own safety, he walked at a brisk pace across the ledge.

Andrea watched him with a certain amount of bewilderment as he headed for the route down from the rocks that Jayne had pronounced unsafe. She recalled his remark about Victoria's death being a local legend, and she imagined the story that would be passed on from one generation to the next.

Where would Holt be then, when white-haired men told their grandchildren the legend of Victoria Carraday? Would he still be living at Ravenspire, by that time a lonely, bitter old man, his daughter grown and gone, Sybil and Carl and John deceased, with only Laura to see after his needs?

Andrea drew in a sharp breath. The idea of Holt as a bitter old man suddenly seemed too real.

No, she told herself. *Someday Holt will remarry. He'll enjoy life again, smile freely, laugh easily. He and his new wife may even have a baby together.*

Abruptly, Andrea rose to her feet. The afternoon no longer seemed gentle. The air had turned cold; it whipped up a frenzy of whitecaps on the water. Andrea turned from the view of the sea and walked back to the stone stairs.

By the time she arrived at the house and went up to her rooms, she felt chilled. She heard the high, whining sound of a vacuum cleaner. Opening the door, she saw Laura pushing a bulky upright sweeper along the carpet by the bed. Laura looked up and promptly turned off the machine.

"Andrea, I'm glad you came just now." Laura unplugged the vacuum and wound the cord around the handle. "When I was dusting, I found a necklace on the floor, half hidden under the corner of the bureau. It must have fallen there after your jewelry box toppled over." She retrieved a chain from the top of the bureau and gave it to Andrea. "It's a precious locket. I'm sure you would've soon missed it."

The words of gratitude froze on Andrea's lips as she stared in disbelief at the heart-shaped pendant.

"Andrea, what's wrong?"

"Nothing," she stammered. A dull pain invaded her temples. "Thank you, Laura," she said absently.

"Are you sure you're okay? You're deathly pale."

"I'm just tired," she managed. "I was out riding this afternoon." She brought a finger up to trace the initial A etched on the front of the locket.

"All right. I'm finished with the cleaning. But if you need me for anything, please let me know."

"Yes, Laura. I will." After Laura was gone, Andrea flopped down on the love seat.

For a long while Andrea stared at the closed locket, turning it over in her hands. How could this have happened when she'd so methodically discarded every memento that might remotely remind her of the past?

She undid the catch on the heart. Alan's face smiled out at her from one side of the locket, her face from the other. With an odd feeling of detachment, she recalled the evening when he had surprised her with the necklace. It had been exactly one month before he'd asked her to marry him.

They'd gone to their favorite French restaurant, a cozy bistro. They'd dined on coq au vin while enjoying the romantic strains of the bistro's five-piece orchestra. Over dessert, Alan had produced the tiny white box tied with a gold ribbon.

Andrea studied the photos again. With his sandy hair skimming the top of his forehead, Alan gave off an almost boyishly handsome appearance. How deceptive appearances could be! She looked very young, too—guileless, she realized. But then, there was no scar to hide.

She sat in lonely silence as she gazed out the window. The color of the sky was deepening from blue to dusky purple. Andrea recalled how Alan's eyes had widened in disgust at the sight of the jagged wound on her cheek.

"You're getting that fixed, aren't you?" he'd asked, leaning over her hospital bed. "Benjamin Weiss—the best plastic surgeon in the city, Andrea. I'll get in touch with his office first thing tomorrow. Oh . . ." His mouth had twitched nervously. "Say, while you're under, why don't you have Doc Weiss straighten out that bump on your nose?"

The implication had been clear. It wouldn't do for successful attorney Alan Grimes's fiancée to have a scar on her face—or a bump on her nose. Alan Grimes's fiancée must be perfect in every way. And who cared about scars that couldn't be excised with a scalpel?

I hope you've found the perfect woman, thought Andrea, viciously clasping the locket shut. She strode with purpose to the wastebasket. Just as she was ready to throw the necklace in the trash, she reconsidered. *What if Laura finds it when she's emptying the basket?* Backing up, she took out her jewelry box from the bureau and shoved the locket deep into a corner, under a jumble of costume pins.

By the time Andrea took her place at the dinner table, the dull throbbing in her head had become a piercing pain that bore through her eye and exited at the base of her skull. The smell of the food Sybil placed in front of her made her sick. For Elizabeth's sake, she kept up a cheerful facade. But as soon as the girl was done eating, Andrea thought only of excusing herself, too.

"Not feeling well tonight, Miss Lane? You've hardly touched your food or drunk a drop of your wine."

Though she hadn't once looked directly at Jayne during the course of the meal, Andrea had known that the old woman was eyeing her. "No, I'm fine," she said. She forced herself to take several swallows of wine, though the drink was apt to make her headache worse. Picking up her fork, she ate two bites of the seafood soufflé on her plate. The second bite felt as if it were stuck in her throat. Another wave of nausea gripped her, and she had a sudden fear that she would throw up all over the fine linen tablecloth.

"I'm sorry . . . excuse me," she mumbled, not caring what Jayne thought as she rose unsteadily to her feet.

The candles seemed to multiply as Andrea stared at them. Six became twelve—or was it twenty? The door to the corridor divided in two; Andrea bumped against the wall on her way out. She reeled down the corridor. The pain was a scalding fire in her head; jagged lines burst like fireworks in front of her eyes.

Here is the foyer. No, a little farther. All the doors are closed. Must be the corridor. The west wing. No, the east wing. Where am I?

A door opened in front of her. Or was it two? Or four? She lurched toward it and staggered into a room that was pitch black except for a small pool of light that spilled in from the corridor.

A blast of cool air blew across her face and forehead as she entered the room. She grasped at the wall with her hand, steadying herself.

Have to rest for a moment, get my bearings. She slumped against the wall. Tilting her head back, she gazed into the soothing darkness. But something was wrong.

Stars twinkled above her. And the moon—a quarter moon. How had she gotten outdoors? She blinked, rubbed her eyes. Were the stars and the moon an illusion? There were so many stars, more than she'd ever seen, even on a summer's night.

The stars began to move in their orbits, throwing showers of sparks into the darkness. Perspiration broke out on Andrea's forehead and beaded on her upper lip.

The stars moved faster, spinning out of control across the night sky. Something else moved. A shadow, the shape of a person. Then it melted into the darkness.

Andrea heard a voice, as if from far away—a husky, masculine voice. "Look up at the ceiling," the voice told her.

"Holt," she whispered hoarsely. Then she knew. She wasn't outside after all. She was in the Grand Hall, and the stars and the moon above were only make-believe. She closed her eyes and hunched against the wall, shivering with pain and cold until sleep overtook her.

Chapter Eleven

The first thing Andrea was aware of when she opened her eyes was that her neck felt stiff, and there was a cramp in her left leg and a soreness around the bones of her eyes.

What time is it? she wondered as fuzzy memories came back to her. She'd had a horrific migraine and gotten lost on her way to her rooms. She'd found an open door and stumbled into a dark place. Now she saw daylight streaming across the floor from a pair of glass doors at the far end of the room. When she looked up, she noticed the tapestry of the blue unicorn hanging above her, and she knew where she was.

She tried to raise herself into a sitting position, but something held her back. With a shock of surprise, she saw two small arms clasped around her waist from behind. "Elizabeth?" she said. There was no response, so she carefully turned until she could see the little girl.

Elizabeth sat up and blinked. She was dressed in a frilly nightgown. "Where are the stars?" the girl asked, staring at the ceiling.

Andrea recalled her own puzzlement on seeing the stars the night before. She followed Elizabeth's gaze. The domed ceiling was just an ordinary ceiling again. "There's a switch on the wall by the door that turns the stars on and off," she explained. "When did you come into the Grand Hall, Elizabeth?" *Were you sleepwalking?* she wanted to ask.

"Probably about midnight. I got hungry and I came downstairs for a cookie."

"And you saw the stars on the ceiling then?"

The girl nodded in response. "I was eating my cookie, and

I saw you on the floor, and I thought you were sick. But you were asleep, and I didn't want you to be alone, so I stayed and went to sleep, too."

That meant Elizabeth must not have been sleepwalking—and that someone had entered the Hall after her and flipped off the light show. Andrea suspected that the person was Jayne. She could almost hear the old woman tattling to her nephew, "I made the most shocking discovery, Holt. Your new tutor, Miss Lane, passed out on the floor of the Grand Hall. Little wonder, with the three glasses of wine she consumed at dinner. Or was it *four?* She virtually staggered out the door. You should dismiss her at once, Holt. . . ."

"I'm not sick," Andrea assured the girl, "but I did have a very bad headache last night." *The worst migraine of my life,* she thought to herself. "The headache made me feel confused. I wandered in here by mistake and fell asleep."

Elizabeth's gaze darted around the room. "I saw the woman," she said at last. "Over there." She pointed to an open area on the other side of the Hall.

"What woman was that?"

"The one who went away."

Andrea's mouth turned suddenly dry. "What did she look like—the woman who went away?"

"She had pretty blond hair and she wore a filmy white dress with roses on it. She was dancing 'round and 'round. She was . . . she was . . ." The girl's hands flew to her face. "She was my mommy!" Elizabeth cried.

Andrea quickly gathered the girl close. As gently as possible, she asked, "You saw your mommy last night?"

"Not last night," the girl said in a whispery voice.

"When then?"

"After she went away," Elizabeth repeated.

Andrea thought of the drawing that she'd believed was Laura. "You showed me a picture you'd drawn of a woman in a flowered dress. Is that your mother, Elizabeth?"

The girl didn't answer, but huge, glistening tears welled in her eyes. "Mommy wouldn't come," she said, hiccuping.

"She wouldn't come to me when I called. She just kept dancing, and then she went through the glass doors, and I never saw her again."

Andrea sat very still while Elizabeth gave way to quiet sobs. There had to be an explanation for what the girl had seen. If Elizabeth had developed a problem with sleepwalking, as Sybil claimed, and had wandered into the Grand Hall one night after her mother's death, she might have been dreaming of her mother, then wakened, believing that the dream was real. Or, Andrea reasoned, since Laura had found her in the Hall, maybe it was a case of mistaken identity. Wasn't it possible that a distraught little girl had, for a moment, seen Laura as her mother and the notion stuck in her mind, embellished with the passing of time into a more lavish tale?

Hadn't the psychiatrist told Holt that suppressed memories might be freed by some event in a person's life? Elizabeth had ventured into the Grand Hall because she saw her tutor there and sensed that something was wrong. Was that enough to trigger vivid—if perhaps inaccurate—images of her mother from the girl's subconscious? Was this the breakthrough Holt had been waiting for for so long?

Elizabeth pulled back. Her eyes were red-rimmed but dry. "Can we eat breakfast now?" she asked hoarsely.

Andrea strove for normalcy as she checked her watch. It was almost eight o'clock. "Yes," she said, "but let's go upstairs and change our clothes first."

On their way out of the Grand Hall, they ran into Laura. The housekeeper gaped in astonishment.

"Andrea! Elizabeth? What on earth...?"

Andrea gave Elizabeth's shoulder a squeeze. "Go on upstairs. I'll see you in the dining room in half an hour."

The girl hesitated. She looked from one adult to the other. Only at Andrea's urging did she finally leave.

Andrea briefly explained to Laura the events of the evening past and how Elizabeth had come into the Grand Hall. She shared the story Elizabeth had told her and confided her own theories as to what the girl might actually have seen.

"It's amazing," Laura said. "No wonder Elizabeth had refused to set foot in the room." She shook her head. "The poor child. Thinking that she saw her mother there. What a terrible shock that must have been for her."

"Laura, do you by any chance remember if you were wearing a white dress patterned with red roses the time you found Elizabeth in the Hall?"

"I don't recall what I was wearing, but I know I've never owned a dress like you just described." She gave a little gasp. "Mrs. Carraday had a dress like that."

"Are you sure?"

"I'm positive." Laura suddenly appeared eager to talk. "Mrs. Carraday had scads of beautiful clothes. She used to go to San Francisco at least every other month. A designer there made all of her clothes for her." She pressed a hand to her forehead. "Oh, I remember now. Mrs. Carraday wore the dress to a cocktail party once. It was an afternoon affair, and she had on a matching white hat with a wide red satin bow. Her hair—it was such a striking shade of blond—fell down over her shoulders in waves. I'm sure she was the envy of every woman at the party."

Laura's voice dropped. "The men were absolutely wild about her. She was so gorgeous—and she flirted like mad whenever she and Mr. Carraday hosted a party. But to me, she seemed remote... untouchable. Do you know what I mean?"

Andrea glanced away. "Yes, I think I do. What happened to her clothes after she passed away?"

"Mr. Carraday gave them to charity, I believe. Yes, I'm certain that's what he did. Andrea..."

"What, Laura?"

"Don't you think the most likely explanation is that Elizabeth saw her mother in the dress before Mrs. Carraday died? She must've remembered that. Then when she was sleepwalking and went into the Grand Hall, she just imagined that her mother was there, dancing. She was at such an impressionable age then. I've heard that memory starts at about the age of three. But Elizabeth was always so perceptive, I wonder if she might be apt to remember more than the average child.''

"I wonder, too." Andrea paused. "Do you know when Mr. Carraday is coming home?"

"I'm not sure. But he's certain to call this evening or early tomorrow. He always does that—always wants to talk with his daughter. He's a devoted father, though to some it might not always appear that way. Holt Carraday is a fine man, Andrea. He deserves far better than..." Suddenly Laura seemed to catch herself, and her tone was slightly distant when she said, "I'm sorry. The morning's half over and I really do need to get my cleaning done. Did you want to speak with Mr. Carraday when he phones?"

"No, I... I'll just wait until he's back." As she watched Laura step into the Grand Hall, carrying her duster and polishing cloths, Andrea knew she had just witnessed an example of the loyalty that Holt so highly valued. At the same time, she longed to call Laura back, to demand to know what it was that Holt deserved far better than.

After they'd eaten breakfast, Andrea asked Elizabeth if she'd like to take the Gull to the small strip of beach in Seacliff. They would fly the kite, then have lunch in the village. She couldn't help noticing how Elizabeth jumped at the chance.

On the drive to town, Elizabeth confided that her favorite place to eat in Seacliff was Lou's Pizza Joint. Andrea's idea of having lunch at The Timbers Café went by the wayside. The girl chattered about the Seacliff Theater—"it only has fifty seats"—and gave an enthusiastic thumbs-up to the re-released *Star Wars*. "I went with John and Laura," she said. Then, giggling, she confessed, "I liked the character of Luke Skywalker best. I think he's cute."

Andrea laughed, relieved to see Elizabeth acting happy and relaxed. She decided she wouldn't make any more mention of the Grand Hall and of what the girl may or may not have seen there four years ago. Given time and patience and—Andrea hoped—a lot of loving attention from her father, Elizabeth might recall other memories of her mother.

They parked in the heart of the village and walked to the beach. But as it turned out, the day was a poor one for the sport of kite-flying. The wind was fickle, rising in bursts, then dying away to a dead calm. After a dozen failed attempts to launch the Gull, Andrea suggested that they might do better to try again after they had lunch.

"Maybe the wind will pick up," she said when she saw the dejected expression on Elizabeth's face.

They strolled along the small strip of beach. Elizabeth skipped ahead of Andrea, crouching every few feet to pick up some object and stuff it in her jacket or jeans pocket.

As she watched the young girl, Andrea recalled the day she, Holt, and Elizabeth had visited the Long Beach Peninsula and flown the Gull on the lovely beach there. Did Holt remember the day as clearly as she did? Or had it faded to a dim memory in his mind? She stared up at the washed-out sky. Soon there would be precious little blue to see. The winter rainy season was fast approaching, when the heavens opened in earnest with a flooding downpour that would rarely slacken until spring.

"Nothing but gray skies for weeks on end," Nanna used to lament over the phone to her granddaughter. *"It's been raining buckets. But if you were here, Andy, instead of in Boston, I wouldn't mind the weather so."*

A sudden feeling of loneliness tore at Andrea's heart. She wouldn't mind the gray skies or the rain either, she decided, if only she could drink her fill of blue in the depths of Holt's eyes.

Desperately she searched her mind for some pearl of wisdom Nanna had shared with her on the subject of love. She realized sadly that Nanna had never given her any counsel on falling in love. Maybe it was because she believed "Andy" was too young to be concerned about such matters.

I'm not too young now, Andrea thought miserably, *and I could use some sage advice. I'm afraid I'm falling in love again with a man who can never return my feelings.*

Elizabeth raced back to where Andrea stood. She proudly displayed the cache of polished stones, shells, and smoothed bits of colored glass that she'd collected. "I always pick out the prettiest stones for Dad," she said. "He keeps them in a big jar in his bedroom."

"That's very nice," Andrea said, perilously close to tears. "Why don't we go for some pizza?"

The weather deteriorated over the lunch hour, and by the time Andrea and Elizabeth emerged from Lou's Pizza Joint, it had started to rain. Andrea drove the Toyota back to Ravenspire with Elizabeth slouched morosely beside her.

They spent the rest of the day reading and playing word and geography games with sets of flash cards that Andrea unearthed from one of the shelves in the classroom. That evening they had their dinner in Andrea's rooms as night closed in on the mansion.

Elizabeth appeared restless. She picked at her food more than ate it and jumped up now and again to peer out the window. "I want it to stop raining," she whined as she settled herself on the love seat for the fourth time.

"I do too," Andrea commiserated, wondering if the girl's mood was really due to the foul weather—or if Elizabeth was troubled by the memory of her mother. Through the window, Andrea saw that the rain had changed over to a fine mist. There was apt to be thick fog by daybreak.

Elizabeth sighed. "I wish I could go riding tomorrow on Patches, but I guess I have to wait a couple more days."

"It's hard to wait, I know." Andrea thought of a possible solution. "How would you like to take a ride on Shadow instead?" she asked.

"You mean I could ride with you? Tomorrow?"

Andrea smiled at the girl's change of mood. "Yes, I don't see why not. Provided that the weather breaks."

True to her own prediction, Andrea woke to fog so thick

that she could barely see the expanse of lawn directly below her windows. But it soon evaporated, revealing a cloudless sky and sunshine. In high spirits, she and Elizabeth set off for the stable barn after breakfast.

There was no sign of Carl around the barn, and so Andrea took down the English saddle and the bridle. The mare acted a little skittish as Andrea adjusted the harness. Shadow shook her head and whinnied, fighting the bit, and Andrea questioned for a moment whether it was wise to take the animal out with two riders on her back. But the mare had proven herself to be gentle, hadn't she? There seemed no reason for undue concern.

"May I lead her to the door?" Elizabeth asked anxiously.

"Here." Andrea handed over the reins.

Shadow briefly resisted Elizabeth's efforts to take the reins. But after the girl had spoken softly to her, the mare calmed down and let herself be led along.

Andrea made a final check of the harness to be certain that it was properly adjusted. She offered a few words to Shadow as she scratched the mare's ears. Then she helped Elizabeth up into the saddle and mounted the animal behind the girl.

Just as she was guiding Shadow toward the West Trail, Andrea saw Carl rounding the corner of the barn. She raised her hand in a wave to him.

Without warning, Shadow snorted and flung her head back and forth. Her eyes shone with a strange, frenzied look. In the next instant, the mare reared on her hind legs.

Acting on instinct, Andrea clutched the reins in one hand and grabbed hold of Elizabeth with the other. "Easy, Shadow! Down!" she said, pulling the reins taut.

The mare responded by violently thrashing her front legs in the air.

Elizabeth screamed, and Carl came running forward with a shout. Andrea's heart pummeled against her rib cage as she gave another command to the mare. Out of the corner of her eye, she saw Carl make a desperate grab for the bit.

"Whoa! Easy, girl!" Carl yelled.

Shadow bucked and charged around Carl in a frantic circle, narrowly missing him as her front hooves plowed the ground. Carl ducked and made another desperate lunge for the harness.

With a wave of sheer black fright, Andrea realized that she was losing her hold on both Elizabeth and the reins. Elizabeth was openly sobbing. She twisted in the saddle, her hands flapping helplessly.

"Put your arms around my neck!" Andrea ordered the girl, and Elizabeth obeyed. Then Shadow gave a bellow, and Andrea felt herself being tossed like a rag doll from the mare's back.

A voice from the past thundered in her ears. It was her father's. *"Fall free from the horse! Fall free!"*

Andrea tucked Elizabeth's head into her chest, shielding the girl's body with her arms as she tumbled to the ground. The world slowed, careened to a screeching stop. As if in a snapshot, Andrea saw the sky above, the sun floating in an azure pool. She heard the distant, pathetic call of a bird. She tried to answer the creature, but couldn't summon the words. Then there was only a smothering blackness that silenced the call and snuffed out the brilliance of the sun.

Someone was drawing her from her dream. The dream was beautiful and terrifying, full of comforting light and horrible darkness. From a distance she smelled the bracing scent of the sea blended with the restful odor of the forest. She struggled to waken, but the dream pulled her back, and she had no will to fight it.

She sat on a majestic white steed, enfolded in the arms of a nobleman with ebony hair and cold blue eyes. They were galloping through space, chasing a cloud, touching a star. The sun was in front of them, blinding them with its light. The moon was behind them, sinking into a ruby sea.

She heard the cry of a bird, and she peered into the sky. A streak of lightning split the clouds in two; a roar of thunder shook the earth beneath the stallion's feet. She looked down and saw that she was clad in a filmy white gown covered in crimson red roses. Gazing into the man's eyes, she gasped. The raven was there, reflected in a sapphire sky. She sensed danger, smelled the scent of blood, tasted it, and her heart beat with a terrible fright.

The nobleman closed his eyes and whispered her name. It was a plea, an oath, a solemn prayer. She was no longer afraid. The danger had passed. Then the nobleman's mouth claimed hers, and as the steed galloped on, she felt herself falling free through time and space.

"Miss Lane."

Her eyes fluttered open; wavering above her was the distorted image of someone's face. She felt drugged, as if she had slept for a thousand years. A dull ache encompassed her head. She concentrated on focusing her gaze, and slowly the face in front of her came into sharper view. The features were kindly, those of an older man, with deep lines around the eyes and a receding gray hairline. The mouth, though, was drawn down at the corners. "Who..." she began to ask, choking on the question.

"I'm Dr. Saunders," a quiet voice said.

"Dr...." Andrea tried to sit up. A wave of dizziness forced her back. She fought a rising wave of panic. *Where am I?* She drew in a shaky breath, and an achingly familiar scent rushed into her nostrils. "Am I...in the hospital, Dr. Saunders?"

"No, but you've been injured, and I suspect you have a slight concussion. I'd like to ask you a few questions," Dr. Saunders continued gently. "Can you tell me your full name and where you are from?"

"Andrea Melanie Lane." She groaned. "From Boston."

"And where do you live, Andrea?"

"Bos... No, Ravenspire."

"Very good, Andrea. What is your profession?"

"I'm..." Her mouth was so dry; she licked her lips to moisten them. "I'm a teacher. A tutor," she amended. She looked at the doctor. His face went out of focus again, like the fuzzy image on a television with poor reception. "Could I have some water, please?"

"Yes, of course."

Andrea saw movement in the shadows beyond where the doctor stood. She heard the sound of water running. Dr. Saunders put an arm behind her and helped her to a sitting position. Then he pressed a glass to her lips, and she took several small swallows of the cold water.

"Do you recall what happened—how you got hurt?" he asked, setting the glass aside.

Andrea closed her eyes and strained to remember. *The dream.* "I fell," she said at last, "from a horse."

"That's right. Anything else?"

"No ... yes." She smiled. "The horse was a white stallion, and we were galloping through space ... trailing a cloud, outracing the wind." There had to be more. But her thoughts refused to jell. Opening her eyes, she saw that Dr. Saunders was smiling, too.

"Not quite, Andrea," he said. "But close enough for the present. Now, if you can sit up for me again, I need to examine your eyes, listen to your heart and lungs, and test your reflexes."

The doctor conducted his exam with an occasional "Hmm" muttered under his breath. He plied her with more questions—whether she had double vision or a headache.

"No double vision, just a dull headache," she said.

When he was finished, he plumped up the pillows behind Andrea and helped her find a comfortable position. "The only other injuries I could find are bruises on your left leg and arm. Your heart sounds healthy and strong and your lungs are clear. Your reflexes are normal. But I do want you to have bed rest for a day or two, and I'll be back tomorrow to check on your progress."

Dr. Saunders made a motion with his hand, and Andrea saw a woman step forward. "Laura," she whispered.

"Laura and I will help you change into some fresh clothes," the doctor said.

"I took a nightgown from your bureau," Laura said.

"But . . . this isn't my bedroom. Where am I?"

"In Mr. Carraday's rooms," Laura said. "In his bed."

"No," Andrea protested. She struggled to sit up. She had to tell Laura and Dr. Saunders that she needed to get back to her own rooms, her own bed.

"Lift your arms up, Andrea," Dr. Saunders ordered.

She lifted her arms. "Please, you have to help me to my bedroom," she said as Laura slipped the sweater off over her head.

"Sorry," Laura replied, "but those are Mr. Carraday's orders. You're to stay here until you've recovered."

"But Ho . . . Mr. Carraday's gone."

Laura smiled as she helped Andrea out of her jeans and into the nightgown. "No, he's home, Andrea—downstairs. He came right away when he heard you'd been injured."

"Andrea." It was Dr. Saunders again. "I'm going to leave some medicine for you." He handed her the glass of water and two capsules. "These will ease any dizziness and pain you may have and help you sleep soundly."

Laura produced a tray with a glass of juice and a muffin, which she set on the bedside table. "In case you wake up in the night and need some nourishment, Andrea. I'll leave the lamp on, too."

Dr. Saunders gathered up his instrument case and followed Laura out of the room.

When they were gone, Andrea fell back on the bed. She pressed her cheek against the pillowcase and pulled the covers up to her chin. Groggily, she vowed to forget that she was in Holt's rooms, lying in his bed. She would rest that night and tomorrow would sneak off to her own bed.

But Holt's unique masculine scent was everywhere, on everything she touched—the satiny pillowcase, the sheets, the blanket and spread. And as she drifted into sleep, a feeling of peace settled over her, like the solace she had found once in Holt's arms.

Chapter Twelve

Like a fretful dream, the memory of her fall from Shadow drew Andrea out of her sleep. She sat up, panting for breath, Elizabeth's name on her lips. *Where are you? Are you all right? Are you even alive?*

Light from a lamp in a corner of the room cast a soft glow across the foot of the bed. The pain in Andrea's head was gone, but there was a sensation of being on a slow-moving merry-go-round, and she moaned as she swung her legs over the side of the bed. She must get up, must find Elizabeth. She put her feet on the floor and took an unsteady step.

A figure appeared from the shadows, and strong hands took hold of Andrea's shoulders. They coaxed her back onto the bed. Holt's unique, masculine scent rushed into her nostrils. Then his face came into view.

"You've had a dream," he said in a low, soothing voice.

"No!" Andrea strained to twist out of his grasp. "Elizabeth . . . the mare . . . I couldn't control her."

"I know." Holt adjusted the pillow behind her head and sat down on the edge of the bed beside her. "Elizabeth's all right."

Out of sheer relief, Andrea gave a choked, desperate laugh. *Elizabeth's all right. She's all right.* And Holt was near, his hands gently massaging her arms. *And all I'm wearing is this flimsy nightgown,* Andrea thought suddenly.

"Yes," he went on, "and she asked about you, too. I told her she might be able to see you tomorrow." He withdrew his hands and glanced at the lamp. Somewhere in the room, a clocked ticked softly. "It's already tomorrow," he said.

Andrea forgot her own self-consciousness for a moment as she studied Holt's face in profile and noticed the rumpled condition of his clothes. His white shirt was open at the collar; a patch of dark curls peeked through. A stubble of beard shadowed his chin, and his hair tumbled recklessly over his forehead. He looked as if he would drop from sheer exhaustion. Had he kept a constant vigil at her bedside?

"How are you feeling?" he said.

"Better. A little thirsty."

"Here's some juice." He picked up the glass of juice that Laura had left and gave it to her.

Their fingers made contact, and his hand lingered on hers momentarily. "Careful," he said.

Careful. The word echoed in Andrea's mind as she took a sip from the glass. She knew that Holt was warning her not to spill juice on herself. But the word held many layers of meaning for her at that moment.

"I don't understand . . ." Andrea shook her head. "I can't think why Shadow threw us off. She was a little nervous when I was putting on her tack. But I dismissed it." Tears welled in her eyes. "It was my fault. I didn't use proper caution."

"Don't!" he said. "Listen to me. You saved my daughter's life. Carl told me what happened, how you turned and made sure that you took the brunt of the fall."

"Then why . . ."

Holt got up from the bed. "Carl found a snake coiled in the grass—only a harmless garter snake, but it was obviously enough to cause Shadow to panic. There was nothing more you could have done. Now drink your juice. You need to rest."

Over the rim of the glass, Andrea saw Holt walk to a chair that was situated in a corner near the bed. After he sat down, she put the half-empty glass aside and closed her eyes, secure in the knowledge that he was close by.

The next time Andrea opened her eyes, she saw that the shadows were gone from the room. Holt was gone, too. The chair he'd occupied was empty and the lamp on the table turned off. Light came in from a window across the room, and when Andrea pushed herself into a sitting position, she glimpsed slate gray sky through the glass.

She saw other things as well. Holt's bed was enormous, with unadorned posts at its foot and head. Opposite the window, a marble hearth was laid with a bank of burning logs. Bookshelves crammed with books were built into the wall, and an old-fashioned armoire took up one corner. A tall glass jar stood on the armoire. Was it the jar that held the treasures Elizabeth gleaned from the beach?

There was only a single painting in the room, an oil rendering of a great ship with furled sails, tacking toward a rocky shore. Despite the stark furnishings, every object Andrea's gaze touched on reminded her of Holt. Maybe it was because the scent of the sea and the forest permeated the room.

I have to get out of here, she thought. Testing her balance, she sat up. She felt so shaky that she had to rest before attempting to throw off the covers and ease her legs over the edge of the bed. She got as far as putting her right foot on the carpet when a knock came at the door.

Hastily, Andrea combed her fingers through her hair and straightened her nightgown. "Come in," she said, steeling herself for a lecture from Holt when he saw that she was attempting to get out of bed.

Instead of Holt, the housekeeper walked into the room. "I see you're up," Laura said with a smile. She was carrying towels in one hand, a small basket in the other.

"I'm feeling better, Laura. I want to get back to my own rooms this morning."

Laura shook her head. "I'm afraid Mr. Carraday wouldn't approve of that. Not yet, anyway. Dr. Saunders will be here in another hour or so to look in on you. In the meantime, I thought you could probably use a little assistance in getting to the bathroom. And I've brought a few personal items that you might appreciate having on hand."

Andrea saw that it was useless to protest, so she let Laura

guide her to the bathroom. The housekeeper handed her the towel set and the basket and said that she would be waiting outside in case Andrea needed any further help.

"I'd like to get dressed," Andrea called through the door. "If you'd bring me a pair of slacks and a blouse from my closet, Laura."

Despite some slight dizziness and an overwhelming feeling of exhaustion, Andrea managed to take a sponge bath. She found her hairbrush, her makeup, and toothbrush and toothpaste in the basket. As she washed and put on her makeup, she studiously tried to ignore the men's grooming supplies that were neatly arranged on the counter by the sink. When she was finished, she repacked the basket and took it with her. The idea of leaving her toiletries next to Holt's on the counter struck her as too intimate.

Laura returned with the blouse and slacks and helped Andrea into them. Trembling from the effort, Andrea leaned on Laura as she made her way back to the bed.

The housekeeper went out but soon came back with breakfast. The food seemed to revive Andrea slightly. She was nibbling on a piece of toast when Dr. Saunders hustled into the room.

Andrea related her memories of the accident to the doctor. "Good," he said. After he examined her, he told her that he was pleased with her progress. He gave her some more medication and cautioned her to rest in bed for a day or two.

"Give yourself time," he advised. "Take it easy when you resume your activities. If you find any of your symptoms worsening, have Holt call my office immediately. Otherwise, you should do fine."

Andrea remembered little of the rest of the day. She dozed off after the doctor left, and the next time she wakened, she saw Holt sitting in the chair. She had no real consciousness of the passing of minutes and hours as she drifted in and out of sleep, though she had an awareness of Holt's presence in the room and of the questions he softly asked her whenever she opened her eyes.

Would she like a drink of water or juice? "Yes," she'd nod. Could he adjust her pillow to a more comfortable position? "Yes," she'd whisper. Once, when she woke up, he asked if his daughter might visit her for a few minutes. "Oh yes, please," Andrea begged, and he smiled at her. She noted that his face was clean-shaven, his hair neatly combed. But the dark circles under his eyes betrayed his lack of sleep.

The reunion with Elizabeth was a poignant one, with the girl crawling onto the bed beside Andrea. They hugged each other, and Andrea assured the young girl that she was going to be all right. But Elizabeth clung to Andrea until her father admonished her that it was time to go.

Gradually, Andrea felt her strength returning. Her mind cleared and the dizziness abated. "What time is it?" she asked, sitting up in bed after yet another snooze.

Holt came over to the bed. "About four—in the afternoon. Are you feeling better?"

Andrea stretched her arms and yawned. "So much better that you'll be able to reclaim your bed tonight."

Holt didn't reply. "Can I get you a cup of tea and a snack?" he asked, looking away from her. "Or maybe you'd like something to read."

"No tea or cookies, thank you, and I'm not sure I'm quite up to reading yet."

"How about if I read to you?"

For a moment Andrea was too surprised to make a reply. Holt Carraday had relinquished his rooms to her and kept a constant watch at her bedside during her recovery. Was he merely playing the part of a concerned employer? Or was his solicitousness the result of a worried conscience? A horse from his stable had thrown her from its back. Was he afraid that she might sue him? Or at least quit her position, like the succession of tutors that had gone before her? That seemed the most logical explanation for his acts of kindness. Then how was she to rationalize the open expression of concern in his eyes when they met hers? Or the way his hands shook as he smoothed the covers around her?

"I'd love to have you read to me," she said at last.

He appeared to relax a little as he pulled the big chair close to the bed and retrieved several books that were stacked on the night table. "Let's see," he said. A twinkle brightened his eyes. "*Three Blind Mice.*" He held up a book. "Or how about *Thirteen at Dinner*?" He waved another book in the air. "Or maybe you're more in the mood for a little Sherlock Holmes."

Andrea gaped at him. "My novels!"

Holt chuckled. "Laura found the books by your bed." He leaned closer. "So you're a fan of murder mysteries."

Andrea lowered her voice to a confidential tone. "Do you know that I have the complete collections of Agatha Christie and Sir Arthur Conan Doyle? Not to mention Ellery Queen, of course, and Mary Higgins Clark."

"Of course." Holt lifted an eyebrow.

Warming to the subject, she went on, "I've read them so many times I have them memorized. Here, let me show you." She snatched *Thirteen at Dinner* from his hands. "I can turn to any page at random and without looking tell you exactly what's written there." She had a reason for picking that particular book. There was a crack in the spine that made the book fall open to a scene that she knew by heart. She flung open the book and gave it to Holt. "The page number?"

"One hundred seventy."

"Hmmm." She pretended to be deep in thought. "I've got it. Poirot has just received a letter from Lucie Adams, in which she defends Carlotta—that's her dead sister—against the dastardly notion that Carlotta was implicated in the murder of Lord Edgware."

"Amazing," Holt said with a grin.

Andrea grinned, too, though she knew that he hadn't been fooled. "Actually, I'm bored by the same old stories," she said. "What do you have here?" She turned to the night table where more books were arranged in a haphazard pile. Selecting a large book near the bottom of the stack, she noted the title on the cover. *The Oxford Book of the Sea.* "Read from this one," she said.

Holt dropped his gaze as he leafed through the volume. "First," he said after searching a while, "a scene from a Stephen Crane story—*The Open Boat.*"

As he read, Andrea thought how well-suited his expressive voice was to the harrowing tale of the four men who'd sailed the doomed steamer *Commodore*.

Holt followed with a long excerpt from Erskine Childers's *Riddle of the Sands*.

Andrea let her mind wander with the reading to faraway lands and seas. But a discordant note threaded through the images, like the urgent clanging of a harbor buoy alerting nearby ships of treacherous waters ahead. Was she, too, facing a threat—one that was just as real as if she were sailing the *Commodore* into a literal gale? The men on the steamer were in danger of losing their lives. But was she in danger of losing her heart to Holt Carraday?

At dinnertime Laura came to the door with two dinner trays. Andrea had expected Holt to retreat to the dining room for the evening meal. The heaped plates of food and steaming cups of tea were proof that she had misjudged his intentions.

Laura set Andrea's tray in front of her. "Elizabeth made this card for you." She handed Andrea a piece of construction paper that was folded in half.

Andrea was touched by the girl's thoughtfulness. The outside of the card was adorned with bright yellow daisies. On the inside there was a message written in small, neat script. *I hope you feel better soon. Love, Elizabeth.*

"We'll be leaving shortly," Laura said, turning to Holt.

"Where are you going?" The question slipped out before Andrea realized that she had no business asking it.

"We're taking Elizabeth to dinner and a movie."

"Lou's Pizza Joint," Andrea guessed. She stared at the card, a smile frozen on her lips. So it would be just Holt and herself, eating alone in his bedroom.

"I want you to know I appreciate all you've done for my daughter," Holt said when Laura was gone.

Andrea's face warmed at the compliment, and she recalled a favor Elizabeth had asked of her. "She said you used to raise rabbits, and she has the idea that if I plead her cause, you'll buy her a replacement for Sylvester."

"She thinks that, does she?" Holt smiled, but didn't commit himself to anything. His expression sobered. "I understand Elizabeth found you in the Grand Hall after you'd had a bad migraine and lost your way."

"Did Laura tell you what Elizabeth claimed to have seen there?" With the anniversary of Victoria's death looming, Andrea asked the question reluctantly.

Holt showed no outward emotion. "Yes." He took a swallow of his coffee. "One thing bothers me about Elizabeth's recollection of her mother."

"What's that?"

"It isn't possible that she saw Victoria wearing the dress she described. After Elizabeth was born, Victoria complained that her figure had changed, that her clothes didn't fit right. She bought a whole new wardrobe, and as far as I can recall, the rose-print dress was shoved to the back of the closet where it stayed until . . ." He gazed down at his coffee cup.

Andrea framed her answer carefully. "Maybe at some point in time Elizabeth saw the dress in the closet and associated it with her mother."

"Could be," was Holt's only response.

The sound of raindrops pelting the windows disturbed the quiet of the room while Andrea discreetly observed Holt. He looked distracted. Was he remembering Victoria in the rose-print dress, her shiny blond hair cascading from under the white hat with the red bow? Or was he thinking of her body, lying on the shore, white and lifeless, after her fall into the sea? Finally, Holt's eyes met hers, and she read in them the plea for a change of subject.

"Would you tell me about Paris?" she said. "All I know is that a certain café there serves Italian cookies."

Holt offered a small, reflective smile. "I'll tell you one story," he said. "A few blocks from the bistro, near a boulevard called the Rue de Rivoli, a street artist had set up his easel. He was trying in his best broken English to persuade every tourist in sight to let him draw their likeness in charcoal. But no one paid him any attention. I guess I must have felt sorry for him, because I agreed to let him do a portrait—on the condition that the subject wasn't me. Naturally, he ended up drawing the Eiffel Tower. I suppose he thought I'd be pleased. But the masterpiece looked more like the Tower of Pisa than Eiffel." Holt made a sketch in the air of the leaning tower. "It turned out better for him than for me. He got paid."

Andrea laughed. "You wouldn't happen to still have the picture, would you?"

"No. At the time, I didn't think it was worth the hassle of stuffing it into my already overpacked suitcase. I guess I should have kept it as a conversation piece."

"Tell me what else you did in Paris, besides support starving street artists."

Holt's expression changed. "In my opinion, Paris is overrated," he said abruptly. "The old cliché is true: Paris is for lovers. I wouldn't recommend visiting the city alone."

Lovers. The word hung in the air between them. *Did you and Victoria visit Paris together?* Andrea wanted to ask. *Did you stay in a cozy, white-curtained hotel room in that most romantic of cities?* A ridiculous surge of envy twisted through her at the thought.

"Well..." Holt rose from his chair and stretched.

Andrea prayed that he was going downstairs to his study. *Work on your model ships. Or make business calls. Or sit and stare into the fire. I don't care. Just don't stay here and make me miserable, wanting you to love me when I know it's impossible.* When he returned, he would find a note on the table, thanking him for his kindness and letting him know that she couldn't deprive him of his bed and another night's rest.

But he didn't leave. Instead, he stacked their empty dishes on the trays and set the trays outside in the hall. Then he returned to his chair.

Since he was obviously in no hurry to go, she wavered between the tactic of pretending that she wanted to fall asleep and the idea that her fragile emotions would be better served by keeping him talking. The silence only heightened her awareness of the fact that she was lying in his bed, within arm's reach of him, and that they were utterly alone in his rooms. She settled on asking him to read to her. That way, she could shut her eyes and turn her face to the pillow without appearing to be rude.

"Anything?" Holt asked.

"More about the sea," she said.

Holt selected first Percy Bysshe Shelley's letter to Captain Daniel Roberts. He moved on to excerpts from James Joyce's *Ulysses* and Ralph Waldo Emerson's *English Traits*. He paused, leafing through the book as if he were hunting for something in particular. His hand stopped on a certain page. " 'The Return,' " he said, "by Swinburne." He began to read the poem slowly, softly. By the time he came to the third stanza, his voice was a whisper, a lullaby.

> " *'I shall sleep, and move with the moving ships,*
> *Change as the winds change, veer in the tide;*
> *My lips will feast on the foam of thy lips,*
> *I shall rise with thy rising, with thee subside.'* "

His voice trailed off, and Andrea opened her eyes. She saw that he was observing her. The clock hammered out the seconds until Holt closed the book that lay in his lap and put it aside. The breath checked in Andrea's throat as she watched Holt take the few steps to her bed and sit down beside her. His gaze locked with hers, and her heart almost came to a thudding halt. As if in a dream, Holt's hand reached up to stroke her hair. Time and again, his fingers tangled then slid through the long, curly strands.

A tremor went through her, and Holt withdrew his hand. His eyes probed hers with wordless questions and looks of unspoken longing. She tried to hide her true feelings from him. In the end, she couldn't. Not with his breath warming her cheek. Not with the scent of the forest and the sea intoxicating her, making rational thought impossible. Not when every fiber of her being ached for his touch.

Once more he began to stroke her hair. The palm of his hand came to rest on her cheek. His fingertips brushed the scar and time ceased to have any meaning. Hazily, Andrea knew that outside the wind was rising. She heard it tear through the ragged limbs of the trees. Perhaps it was the harshness of the sound that brought her to her senses. Or maybe it was the gentleness with which Holt's fingers were exploring the rough flesh of the scar that made her turn away with a strangled cry. But Holt's hand took firm hold of her chin, forcing her to look at him. He pushed her hair back from her cheek, exposing the scar.

"Who did this to you?" He bit out the words.

The story tumbled from her lips. "A... man attacked me," she said in a shaky voice. "I was on my way to a parking garage. It was a winter evening; the streets were empty. The man wanted money and jewelry. When he saw how little I had to offer him, he went into a fit of rage and pulled me into an alley. He put a knife to my throat. I thought he was going to kill me. Instead... he slashed my cheek."

Tears sprang in her eyes as she told Holt the rest of the story—the man's sudden flight from the scene; the patrol car that came by minutes too late; the fruitless search for the mugger; the horrible wailing noise of the siren as the ambulance carried her to the hospital.

"I still shudder every time I hear a siren," she admitted. "Two weeks later, the man attacked another woman. That time he wasn't so lucky. He was wounded when he fired on a police officer. I was told that he bled to death on the way to the hospital."

All the while she was talking, Holt was caressing her

cheek, her hair. When she finished, he dropped his hand and said, "There's more, isn't there?"

"I... was engaged to be married," she said. "He was—is—a successful attorney. Every woman I knew told me how lucky I was to have caught the eye of Alan Grimes. It wasn't until after the attack, when I was in the hospital, that I started to see certain... traits in Alan that I'd always rationalized away in the past. Instead of offering me the sympathy I needed, Alan told me that I was stupid for being out alone, that I was almost... asking to be mugged." She swatted at a tear with the back of her hand. "He also expected me to have not only the scar fixed, but my nose, too. He said he'd never liked the shape of it."

Holt tenderly traced the line of her nose. "What on earth was he thinking?"

"That my nose—that *I* wasn't perfect enough to suit him. I realized that his vision of me and who I actually *am* were poles apart. I was going to have surgery on the scar, but..." She shook her head. "I contracted an infection, and the doctor said the operation would have to wait. I'd already missed too many days at school. I was anxious to get well and resume teaching. Not long after that, I heard rumors that the school would be closing, and I put the surgery on hold indefinitely."

"And your impending marriage?"

"I put that on hold forever. Ironically, Alan had given me an engagement ring a week before the attack. But I forgot to wear it the day I was mugged. So Alan got his ring back, at least."

Holt's eyes projected only the greatest compassion and warmth. How could she have ever thought of them as cold? With a soft groan, he gathered her into his arms. Then he began to kiss away her tears, and she saw that something more than the desire to give comfort blazed in his eyes.

His fingers sought her scar with a sort of feverish urgency. His lips traced a fiery, healing trail along the jagged line. Gasping, Andrea quivered against his lean, muscular body as he held her tighter in his arms. Her hands twined around his neck, and she laced her fingers in the glory of his hair. He kissed her ear, the tip of her nose. Then his lips possessed hers, hungry and searching.

Andrea sagged back on the pillow, and Holt followed. His heart thundered against hers, while outside the storm pounded the windows with rain. Giving herself up to the ecstasy of his kiss, she was carried away by its power to that deserted isle where lonely Crusoes build their boats. She was riding the white steed, laughing, the wind fingering her face. She was chasing a cloud, touching a star. She imagined she saw the mythical raven of her dreams, its wings spanning the blue heaven of Holt's gaze. Holt's eyes shone with a radiance she hadn't seen before. Then his mouth reclaimed hers, and she sensed that they had entered a paradise of their own making.

Without warning, Holt broke the kiss, and the fragile paradise was lost. He pulled away from her with a moan and dragged a hand through his hair. For a moment, Andrea was too dazed to respond. All she could hear was his ragged breathing; even the wind had died away. Then she started to reach out to him, to grasp for the right words to say.

In that instant the quiet was shattered by a desperate and terrible scream that shook the halls of Ravenspire and chilled Andrea's bones to their marrow. Holt jumped up from the bed and charged into the corridor. Another scream brought Andrea fully to her senses. Disregarding Dr. Saunders's orders, she raced out the door after Holt.

Chapter Thirteen

Andrea didn't catch up to Holt until he'd entered the corridor of the west wing. A series of high-pitched screams came from the direction of the Grand Hall, and Holt began to run toward the double doors, which were standing open. Andrea hung back a little, partly from a feeling of weakness in her legs, partly because she thought that if Holt saw her, he would order her to return to bed.

At first, Andrea was afraid that Elizabeth was in the Grand Hall, crying out in fright. But the voice didn't sound like a child's. Besides, wasn't Elizabeth at the movies with John and Laura?

Just as Holt reached the double doors, the figure of a woman emerged from the Hall and brushed past him. Andrea halted in her tracks. A feeling of icy fear gripped her heart at the sight of the woman bearing down on her. Surely the woman was an apparition—or a trick of Andrea's mind induced by her morbid curiosity about Victoria Carraday and fueled by her feelings for Holt. How else could she explain the woman's resemblance to Victoria—the filmy, rose-print dress that rustled seductively around the woman's ankles as she walked and the long, blond hair that tumbled over the woman's shoulders?

Andrea's own body betrayed her at that moment—her lips still tender from Holt's kisses, her legs shaky and weak, not from injury or fear, but from the potent power of Holt's caresses and the shock of his sudden withdrawal from her. She saw that Holt, too, stood without moving, watching the specter of his late wife retreat down the hall.

The woman's head was bowed, her face hidden in shadow until the moment she stopped in front of Andrea. When she lifted her chin, it was Andrea who screamed. Blue eyes burning with hatred and condemnation met Andrea's. As quick as lightning streaking from a cloud, the familiar cane was produced from the voluminous folds of the dress. Andrea ducked just in time as the cane came whipping past her head. In the next instant, Andrea saw that Jayne Evernham was gone and Holt was by her side.

"Get back upstairs and lock yourself in your rooms!" he ordered. His voice shook and his face was pale.

Jayne sprinted into the other corridor, the rose-print dress billowing behind her like a sail in the wind. Holt hesitated only an instant before giving chase.

Not about to leave Holt alone to face the wrath of his mad aunt, Andrea ran after him.

Sybil, who must have been wakened by the ruckus, almost collided with Andrea in the middle of the foyer. Clad in her nightgown, she tagged after Andrea, gasping, "Heaven help us!"

Halfway down the corridor of the east wing, the blond wig came flying off Jayne's head. She didn't look back, but kept going, with her nephew on her heels. At the entrance to the study, she stopped and faced Holt. She made a violent pass at him with her cane, and he barely dodged out of harm's way.

"You and *Miss* Lane!" The old woman struck the air again with her cane. Her face was a mask of rage, the blue eyes glazed and rimmed with red. "Couldn't wait, could you, Holt, to claim her heart, too. Poor Victoria!" she cried. "Poor Victoria!"

Holt's expression was hidden from Andrea as he grabbed Jayne's arm and attempted to take the cane from her. The old woman wiggled out of his grasp and sped through the door of the study.

There was a sickening crash from inside. Andrea rushed forward, her stomach clenched with dread.

Rounding on her, Holt warned, "Stay back!" before plunging into the room after his aunt.

Andrea followed close on his heels. Near the door lay one of the miniature ships, its hull smashed to bits in a sea of broken glass.

By this time, Jayne had retreated to the other end of the room. She brandished the cane as Holt closed in on her. She raised it high in the air and brought it crashing down on a table crowded with glass cases. The cases and their contents went flying against the wall, smashing into thousands of pieces.

"Your ships, Holt! See, your beautiful ships," the old woman taunted. "You love them more than you ever loved Victoria, don't you? Confess it, Holt!" she hissed. "What about your little red-haired girlfriend? Do you love *her?*" She waved the cane in Andrea's direction. "Or will your evil ways drive her to take her life, too?"

A feeling of unreality crept over Andrea. She felt the cook's rough hand clutching hers, heard Sybil's voice still chanting, "Heaven help us." She sensed that Holt was willing her to look at him, but she didn't meet his eyes. All she could do was watch Jayne wield her weapon of destruction, sending more ships to their doom.

"You broke the statue, didn't you?" she said. "And you made Elizabeth believe that you were her mother by dressing in Victoria's clothes and dancing in the Grand Hall."

"Ha!" Jayne spat. "The vixen is smart, too. You'd better tread carefully, Holt, or you might be the one who jumps next."

He didn't respond to the old woman's tirade as he approached her. "Let me have the cane now," he said.

Jayne laughed bitterly. "Give you my dearest friend, my most prized possession?" She lunged at him with the cane time after time as if it were a sharp-edged sword. Her eyes glowed with a look of insane pleasure. Then, unaccountably, the expression of rage began to drain from her features. Her face lost its flushed appearance, the flesh turned pasty white around the garishly painted lips and cheeks. The fire in her eyes flickered out, like the dying flame of a candle that had burned too low. The hand that held the cane trembled.

Jayne began to retreat from her nephew. "Don't come after me," she said, but the threat sounded strangely hollow.

No one moved or said a word while Jayne Evernham wove her way uncertainly between the tables. Even Sybil had quit her chanting, though she didn't let go her death grip on Andrea's hand. In the quiet, Andrea heard once more the rain drumming on the windows of Ravenspire.

Jayne stumbled to the desk; the cane fell from her hand with a clatter. "I'm ... very tired," she said. Her footsteps faltered as she neared the hearth. She steadied herself by leaning heavily on the mantel. Her hair had come loose from its pins. It hung in thick, gray ropes around the haggard face. Jayne's stature seemed suddenly diminished. Her shoulders were hunched; her free arm hung lifelessly at her side.

"I was a great dancer," she said with a feeble sweep of her arm. "And Victoria was a famous actress. We had a bond. We ... understood each other. I loved her. I *loved* her as my *own* daughter."

Jayne stared blankly around the room. Her attention focused for a moment on the doorway, and a smile flickered across her lips as she stretched out her arms in a gesture of supplication. "I didn't let them forget you!" she sobbed. "I didn't let any of them forget you."

"Aunt Jayne ..." Holt came forward and offered her his hand.

"No!" She shrank from him. "Don't touch me." Her gaze darted from her nephew to Andrea to Sybil. "I took good care of Elizabeth—the dear, misguided child." Jayne swayed on her feet. "I ... did it ... for you," she whispered as she crumpled in a heap to the floor.

Holt crouched over his aunt. "Call for an ambulance," he ordered the cook. His glance touched briefly on Andrea. "And please tell them to turn the siren off before they come in the drive."

Andrea knelt by Holt on the floor. Jayne's eyes were half open and fixed in a stare. Saliva bubbled from between the painted lips. "Is she . . ."

"Dead?" Holt looked up. "No, there's a weak pulse."

After that, things happened very quickly. At the sound of voices in the hallway, Holt sent Andrea out to intercept his daughter and John and Laura. Elizabeth was excited to see Andrea, so it seemed natural for Andrea to suggest they go upstairs together. Over Elizabeth's head, Andrea sent Laura and John an urgent signal to go to Holt's study.

Some time later, after she'd patiently listened to Elizabeth's account of her trip to town, Andrea helped the girl to prepare for bed. She hugged Elizabeth close as they said their good nights, then she sat in the same chair Jayne had once occupied to spin her scary stories. Andrea told the girl a gentle tale filled with goodness and hope that she'd heard years ago at Nanna's knee. She didn't leave the room until she was certain Elizabeth had fallen asleep.

When Andrea went back downstairs, she learned that Jayne Evernham was en route to the nearest large hospital, some fifty miles away, and that Holt was following the ambulance in his car. Laura suggested that there wasn't apt to be news on Jayne's condition until morning.

"Are you okay, Andrea?" the housekeeper said with a frown. "You shouldn't be on your feet."

"I'm doing fine, but I think I'll go to bed now."

Laura put her hand on Andrea's arm. "I was afraid it would eventually come to something like this," she said in her gentle manner. "I feel so bad for Mr. Carraday. As long as I've known him, he's always tried to do the fair and equitable thing in every circumstance. He did the best he could to accommodate his aunt. But in recent years, she just got more and more . . . contrary. She wouldn't let any of us come near the Raven's Roost. I wonder . . ." Laura shook her head. "You do need your rest, Andrea. I'd advise you to just sleep in tomorrow."

"You're right. I will."

"Sleep well," the housekeeper said. "Oh, and I'll let you know as soon as we hear a word from Mr. Carraday."

Andrea started off, but her steps slowed as she thought of something Laura had said. Jayne Evernham wouldn't let anyone come near the Raven's Roost. Then it couldn't have been Laura at the window of the tower the day Holt showed Andrea around the estate; it had been Jayne in her blond wig, observing the new tutor with spiteful eyes as perhaps she thought Victoria would have done if she were alive.

It was almost noon by the time Andrea roused herself from bed. She'd lain awake until nearly dawn, then fallen into a deep sleep. A note from Laura was waiting for her, propped on the bureau. According to the brief message, Mr. Carraday had come home early in the morning with the news that his aunt had suffered a major stroke. The doctor's prognosis was guarded. If she survived, Jayne Evernham would be completely paralyzed on her right side, and she would never regain her ability to speak.

The note continued.

Mr. Carraday spent considerable time with his daughter this morning. He feels that it would be best if Elizabeth gets away for a couple of days, and so he's arranged for John, Elizabeth, and me to visit Newport (Oregon). None of us has been to the big marine exhibit there, but we hear it's something to see. Mr. Carraday was disappointed he didn't have the chance to talk with you before he left again for the hospital. But he didn't want to disturb your rest. It's been a trying time for all of us. Take care of yourself. We'll see you on our return.

Best Regards,
Laura

Andrea folded the note and laid it aside. There was a covered tray on the bureau. Lifting the lid, she found a sandwich and fruit and wedges of cheese. A small carafe held tea that was still hot. She ate without tasting, contemplating her future.

It was clear to her that she had to leave Ravenspire. She and Holt had crossed a boundary that should never have been crossed, and there could be no going back to the way things had been in the beginning. For one glorious moment she had allowed herself to believe that there were no longer any barriers between them and that he was perhaps, after all, the knight in shining armor come to capture her heart. She had at last trustingly accepted his show of tenderness and compassion as genuine; she had reveled in his kisses. Had she been so wrong in her judgment of him and his motives? She smarted inside whenever she thought of how he had coldly drawn away from her. And she recalled something Maggie had told her.

"A man has certain ... needs, don't you know," the waitress had remarked.

Had Holt only been giving in to his "needs" when he'd held her in his arms and kissed her? His murmured words of love had sounded so genuine, breathed against her lips. But had they been just words without substance?

If only Nanna were alive! Andrea would entrust herself to her grandmother's gentle care until she felt strong—and wise—enough to make decisions about her future. But Nanna had been dead for many years, and Andrea knew she must focus her energies on the plan she had formulated in the dark, lonely hours of the night. With everyone away from Ravenspire except for Sybil, she would be able to carry out the investigation she hoped would yield some sort of clue that could help piece together the circumstances surrounding Victoria's death. She suspected the key lay in the Raven's Roost. If she did find some answers, then at least Holt might be freed from his burden of doubt and guilt.

Physically, she felt much better than she had the day before, and she didn't waste any time in traversing the corridors to the Raven's Roost. The door was standing wide open, and as Andrea entered the tower, she saw that it had three levels.

Light streamed down on her from a door standing open at the very top. The light drew her like a beacon, and she mounted the several flights of steps.

Until the moment that Andrea stood on the threshold of the room, she hadn't allowed herself to dwell on the fact that she was an intruder in Jayne's private quarters. Never mind that the old woman was gone for good. When Andrea realized that what she saw with her eyes was more a shrine to Victoria Carraday's memory than a room, she almost fled.

Finally, she forced herself to go in. The first thing she took note of was the pictures—black-and-white candids and color photographs—that covered the walls. Some were glamor photos, others the work of an amateur. All of them showed a beautiful young woman with long, blond hair, luminous hazel eyes, and a perfect cupid's-bow mouth.

Then there were the elegant, slim dresses and matching hats that hung on racks and pegs throughout the room. Andrea moved among the racks, touching the several dresses, feeling the textures of the silk, wool, and linen fabrics.

She began to notice other things: a pair of frayed ballet slippers, pieces of jewelry, and picture albums that were stacked on tables and strewn over the floor. She found a ring of keys hanging on a hook—keys that Jayne had used to slip in and out of the locked rooms of Ravenspire? There was something else, a journal lying open, with a single line scrawled across a page that was dated the twentieth.

This is the day my nephew and his new dalliance must pay for their wicked deeds, it said.

"And vengeance is Jayne Evernham's," muttered Andrea under her breath. Leafing back through the journal, she saw that most of the recent entries were illegible. But two stood out, and she managed to read them. In one, Jayne boasted of her intention to *"make a fool of Miss Lane by slipping a pinch of my sleeping powders into her wine tonight."* The entry was dated the seventeenth—the day Andrea had gotten the migraine. No wonder she'd become ill and disoriented! Jayne had doctored her wine with sleeping medication.

Andrea shuddered to think what the results might have been if she'd drunk the whole glass of wine.

The second entry was dated a week after Andrea had arrived at Ravenspire.

Miss Lane is different than the others, Victoria. They were nasty little cowards, and I soon had them on the run. Silly girls! But this one ... I see the way Holt looks at her. If I don't act soon, he will have Miss Lane as his new bride. I vow to stop him!

Andrea closed the journal and placed it on the table where she had found it. There was no need to read any more. She moved on to a pile of albums and chose the thickest one. Playbills and postcards from exotic locales were pasted almost carelessly on the yellowed pages. The playbills—from theaters in and around London—prominently featured the names Dane Clifton and Victoria Sanson. On the next to the last page of the album was a large clipping from a newspaper, a color photograph of a man and a woman standing with their arms wrapped around each other. They were smiling. The woman was Victoria. With a shock of recognition, Andrea realized that Victoria's companion was a younger version of the silver-haired man she had talked to on the Rocks of Destruction. Stunned by her discovery, she read the caption below the photo.

Fun in the sun on the French Riviera for Dane Clifton and Victoria Sanson, stars of the long-running "Opus."

Dane Clifton. Andrea had met the actor face-to-face and not even been aware of it. He must have been putting on the performance of his life for her—pretending to be a tourist, asking her in a mildly interested way about his own lover's death! Had he traveled from England just to visit the Rocks of Destruction on the anniversary of Victoria's death? Had he been to the site before? Did *he* somehow hold the key to what happened that day five years ago?

Studying the picture again, Andrea was struck by another thing that was both strange and disturbing. Elizabeth bore a certain resemblance to the young Dane Clifton. Was it only a coincidence? Surely, Elizabeth was Holt's child, wasn't she? Or had Dane and Victoria—? Andrea breathed a prayer that her suspicions weren't true as she tore the photograph from the page and shut the album.

She knew it might be a long shot, but she had to go back to the Rocks of Destruction. Dane Clifton had paid at least one visit to the place that week. Today was the twenty-first— the date of Victoria's fatal fall. If he returned to the scene, Andrea wanted to be there. As she ran down the winding steps of the Raven's Roost, she formed another silent prayer, asking that if Dane Clifton was hiding secrets about his lover's death, she would be the one to pry them out of him.

The waves roared against the half-hidden rocks below as Andrea emerged onto the shelf high above the ocean. At first glance it appeared she was alone. But when she saw the solitary, silver-haired man standing on the crag, her mouth went dry and her heart gave a lurch in her chest.

Appropriately, the actor was dressed in the color of mourning. In his arms he held a bouquet of crimson red roses. The blooms looked like drops of blood against the dark background of his sweater.

Andrea slowly approached him. He was partially turned away from her, and his stance gave no indication that he was aware of her presence. She stopped a few yards behind him and watched as he bent on one knee and tossed the bouquet of roses over the side of the promontory. Then, as if he'd known all along that she was there, he leapt to his feet and pivoted toward her.

"So... we have the pleasure of meeting again, Miss Lane," he said with an insincere smile.

She stepped forward. "I believe we do, Mr. Clifton."

The green eyes squinted at her. "You know me?"

"You're a famous actor, aren't you?"

He gave a self-deprecating laugh. "How old are you, Miss Lane? I haven't set foot on an American stage in over a decade. Ah! Maybe you saw me as Hamlet at the Memorial

Theatre in Stratford-upon-Avon? Or with the Bramwell Players at the Royal Exchange in London?"

"No," she confessed. She handed him the news clipping which she'd concealed in her sweater pocket.

A look of astonishment flickered over his features as he stared at the picture of himself and Victoria. "Where did you get this?"

"I found it among the personal effects of a woman who ... used to live at Ravenspire."

"You live there now?" the actor said.

"I'm employed there as Elizabeth Carraday's tutor." She studied his face for any change in expression at the mention of the girl's name.

The actor merely gave a sigh. "What a pity that a titian-haired beauty should be closeted away in Carraday's moldy manse." He regarded her shrewdly. "Now that we know I'm a famous actor and you're a tutor who's come into possession of a very old tabloid photo of myself and Victoria, what do you want with me?"

"The mystery of her death has never been cleared up, Mr. Clifton. I suppose I'm curious as to why you've come here on the fifth anniversary of her fatal fall."

"To pay my respects, of course. Why shouldn't I?"

"I'm sure that would be natural, since you loved her."

"Love?" He gave an impatient shrug. "How much do you know about love, Miss Lane?"

His question cut to the quick. She stared down at the water. The sea looked black and foreboding under a brooding sky. "More than you might assume," she replied softly. "There are others who cared about Victoria, others who will never be able to reconcile themselves to her death unless they learn what actually happened that day."

"You mean Holt Carraday, the lord and master of Ravenspire. Do you think that *I* am reconciled to Victoria's death?"

"Would you be here now, if you were?"

"So then, are you playing the detective, Miss Lane? What insight do you expect to gain from me?"

A blast of wind howled around the ledge, and a fine rain started to fall from the sky. Andrea shivered.

"The truth about how your lover died—if you know," she said when the wind faded.

"Ah, the truth!" The actor gazed toward the horizon. " 'Truth sits upon the lips of dying men,' said the great Matthew Arnold. Even if I knew the truth, why should I share it with you?"

"To clear your conscience might be a good start."

He didn't answer her. After a moment, he began to pace. Andrea watched as he prowled along the rock shelf, coming ever closer to the edge with each pass until his feet appeared to teeter half on the rock, half in thin air.

Acting more on instinct than thought, Andrea rushed forward. "No, don't!" she pleaded.

The actor jerked around. "So now you are worried about me slipping to my death, are you?" he said angrily. "Didn't I tell you to guard your step? Or were you imagining that I was about to take a lover's leap?"

Andrea shrank back. She felt foolish, like a child who'd been reprimanded. She could see that he wasn't as near to the edge as she'd judged. Peering cautiously over the side, she saw a splotch of red on the dark rocks below. It was one of the roses from his bouquet. The next rush of water over the rocks washed the flower out to sea.

"This isn't the first time you've visited this spot, is it?" she guessed. "It's very isolated—romantic, too—an ideal place for lovers to meet in secret."

"You're a persistent woman, Miss Lane."

"But it was you, Mr. Clifton, who said that truth sits upon the lips of dying men. Yet only men who are alive can confess their past deeds."

He bowed his head. After what seemed an eternity, he began, "Victoria had written to me, begging to see me. I was at my summer home in the Cotswolds."

It was raining in earnest now. The actor pushed wet, silver strands of hair out of his eyes. "My love for Victoria, hers for me was—how can I put it? Quite frankly, we were addicted to each other. The addiction didn't end with her ill-fated marriage to Carraday."

"So your addiction drove you to come here?"

The actor laughed. "Oh, but I was careful, Miss Lane. I rented a room at a seedy motel a safe distance from the manse. Victoria had given me . . . instructions on how to find this place." He tilted his face to the sky. "It was raining mercilessly. But we were together. That's the important thing, wouldn't you agree?"

"Did she intend to return with you to England?"

"Come now. There's no use sacrificing your health for the sake of curiosity." He held out his hand to her. "My car's parked not far from here."

"I'm not as sickly as you might think," she retorted, fearful he was grasping at an excuse to derail the conversation.

The rain came in sheets, assaulting the actor's face and streaming down his face like tears. "Don't you see? *I* was responsible for Victoria's death."

"How is that possible when you loved her?" Andrea shouted above the shrieking wind.

"You misunderstand. It was *her* love for *me* that drove her to an act of desperation."

"Victoria took her own life?"

"Is that what I said, Miss Lane?"

"It's what you implied."

Dane Clifton suddenly seized hold of her hand. Before she could utter a complaint, he propelled her toward the stairs. He steered her down the steps, then pulled her along a gravel path to a spot where the way opened out onto a clearing. A black Mercedes, its windows darkly tinted, was parked near a spruce tree.

"Make a dash for it," he ordered her. Once they were inside the car, he turned the engine on.

Andrea started trembling, despite the warmth from the

heater vents. "Was it cold the day Victoria died?" she asked through chattering teeth.

"Beastly cold," he responded. His long, pale fingers shook as they curled around the steering wheel. "After we'd held each other for some time, Victoria suddenly broke away, crying. Then she told me we must never meet again."

"What made her change her mind?"

"I believe her sense of duty prevailed over love. She had wired me, telling me to stay in England. The telegram missed by an hour. I was on my way to Heathrow."

"Then you think it was because of Elizabeth that she had second thoughts?"

He bowed his head. "Victoria adored her daughter, though she wasn't ideally suited to motherhood. There was no question in my mind that the child would come with us."

A terrible tightness gripped Andrea's insides. In that instant, she almost hated Dane Clifton and Victoria Carraday. "I couldn't help noticing that..." She averted her gaze. "Elizabeth bears a certain resemblance to you."

"You observed that, did you? I can see the wheels going round in your head. 'Is he? Could it be possible?' I won't answer you."

After a strained silence, he said, "I'm not a religious man, but I've been compelled to wonder if Victoria's death was some sort of divine retribution for my wicked ways."

"You mean because you couldn't stop loving her?"

All of a sudden, he grasped her arms. "You must listen to me, Miss Lane. Victoria would have married me in the blink of an eye. She wanted—no, she desperately needed—the sense of security that she foolishly believed came with saying the vow 'I do.' Unfortunately, the words marriage and commitment have never been in my vocabulary, and so she ran straight into Carraday's arms when the opportunity presented itself. Forgive me, Miss Lane." He released her and fell back against the seat.

"I suppose the years mellowed me," he said. "At any rate, I was ready to make a commitment to Victoria. But I'd waited too long. She knew Carraday would never give up the child, that he would fight for custody to the bitter end. Was there a single doubt in her mind as to which she would choose—Elizabeth or me? In my frustration and anger, I strode to the edge of the crag. I never meant to jump. But the stone was wet and . . . I began to slip."

Andrea gasped. "She thought you were going to jump!"

"Victoria came tearing toward me—just as you did—crying for me to stop. When I realized her purpose was to save my life . . ." He covered his eyes. "She lost her footing. I made a desperate grab for her. It was too late."

"Why didn't you go to the authorities?"

He looked at her. "You think they would have believed me? Or that Carraday would have welcomed me with open arms for bearing the news of his wife's death?"

"It would have been better than . . . turning coward!"

"You brand me as a murderer, then a coward."

"I won't consider you either one if you go to the police now and tell them what you just told me."

He put up his hands. "No."

Their gazes met in brief, silent conflict. Finally, Dane Clifton blinked. His eyes gleamed with unshed tears. "Enough of this," he said in a voice that sounded more weary than gruff. "I'm taking you home to Ravenspire, Miss Lane."

Andrea was too cold and exhausted to raise an objection as he set the car in motion and drove off.

Chapter Fourteen

When Holt hadn't returned home from the hospital by noon the next day, Andrea decided she would drive to Seacliff and have lunch at The Timbers Café. She couldn't stand the feeling of isolation that came from knowing she was almost entirely alone in the mansion.

After a restless, dream-filled night, she had tried to sleep in that morning. But she'd kept thinking of her conversation with Dane Clifton, wondering if there was anything she could have said that would have persuaded him to go to the authorities with his story of how Victoria had died. She kept torturing herself, too, with the question of whether Elizabeth was by birth his daughter instead of Holt's. Hadn't his refusal to tell her directly been as good as an admission that he was Elizabeth's father?

Had Holt been trying to reconcile himself all these years to the possibility that he wasn't Elizabeth's natural father? There was no longer even a shadow of a doubt in Andrea's mind that Holt was devoted to Elizabeth. But was it reasonable to think that the resemblance between the girl and Dane Clifton had slipped Holt's notice? Had he deliberately shut out of his mind any doubts about why Elizabeth didn't share more of his physical characteristics?

Dragging herself from the bed, Andrea dressed for the weather—slate gray skies and the threat of more rain. A few minutes later, a subdued and sad-eyed Sybil delivered a breakfast tray to Andrea and left, saying only, "I'll be in the kitchen if you need me, Miss."

After eating the simple meal of hot cereal, fruit, and tea,

Andrea went downstairs. She walked with purpose through the foyer and along the corridor of the east wing. Since the night of Jayne's tantrum and stroke, she hadn't mustered the courage to visit the study. It was something she needed to make herself do now.

As she'd anticipated, the room was tidy and clean. The broken glass and shattered ships were gone. But it was as if the sparkle had gone out of the room, and the polished tables looked bare without their usual complement of ships.

So much beauty and hard work destroyed, thought Andrea as she moved about the room, touching a glass case here and there that had, by some miracle, escaped Jayne's vengeance. She stopped beside the desk, her gaze arrested by the sight of a model ship that lay on its side near a pot of brown paint.

Andrea recognized the miniature by its sail, and she had to smile at the idea that Holt had used the piece of rice paper that she'd plucked from the trash. She ran a finger along the crinkled edge of the sail, grateful that the tiny ship had been left intact.

On the other side of the desk sat the piece of driftwood that Elizabeth had found on the beach below Cape Disappointment Lighthouse. Andrea recalled Holt's promise to his daughter. If the wood wasn't too soft, he'd said, he would carve a model from it of his great-grandfather's ship, the *Raven*. Would he follow through on his promise? Or had he lost the heart for building ships that sailed on make-believe seas?

I'll never know, Andrea told herself, *because I'll soon be leaving Ravenspire forever.* A choked sob rose in her throat, and she ran from the room before she could give way to tears.

Though it was past the noon hour, The Timbers Café was crowded with diners as Andrea wove her way to an empty booth. She saw with a stab of disappointment that the blond-haired waitress was serving the patrons, and she wondered if it was Maggie's day off again.

Then she heard a familiar voice calling, "Hello, dear," and

she looked up to find Maggie rushing toward the booth with a menu tucked under her plump arm.

There was an awkward moment when the waitress fumbled with the menu. She clucked softly and patted a stray hair back in place.

"Have you heard the news?" Maggie asked breathlessly, shoving the menu under Andrea's nose.

"News?"

"It's all over town. Oh..." Maggie's cheeks flushed. "You don't live in town. How are things going for you? You're still out at that spooky old mansion, aren't you?" She shook her head. "My, will Mr. Carraday be in for the shock of his life when he learns what happened this morning."

Andrea automatically tensed. "What did happen, Maggie?"

"I can tell you, dear, that everyone's sympathies are more with *him* than they were before. Who would've guessed?" Maggie's hands fluttered in the air. "Oh, Patty!" She made a frantic gesture in the direction of the blond waitress who was rushing by with a tray of food. "Be a sweetheart and cover my other tables for me, and the tips are yours."

"Whatever," Patty said with a shrug and a curious glance in Andrea's direction.

Maggie slid into the booth opposite Andrea. "That actor," she said, leaning forward in a familiar way, "the one Mrs. Carraday had an affair with—Danny Clifton or something like that was his name—well, a couple of our local fishermen found his body washed up on the very beach where *hers* was discovered five years ago. A horrible and strange thing, isn't it, dear?"

Andrea's heart gave a sickening lurch as Maggie prattled on without waiting for a reply.

"... rumor is that there was some sort of letter pinned to his clothes—wrapped up in plastic so that it wouldn't get wet. The coroner has to make it official, but with the passport they found alongside the letter, it's almost a certain bet that the body's Mr. Clifton's. I expect the contents of the letter'll leak out even before Sheriff Jackson calls a press conference. He always calls a conference when there's something big going on. We have just the one local paper, and it prints only on Saturdays. I wager they'll put out a special edition for this, though."

Andrea's hands felt cold, her palms cold and clammy. "When did they—the fishermen—find the body?"

"Just a few hours ago. Dear, are you all right? You look ill."

"I... I've been a little under the weather the past few days."

The waitress's eyes narrowed. "Mr. Carraday's treating you decently, isn't he?"

"Yes, he is. That isn't the problem, Maggie."

"I know. It's living out there in that spooky old mansion. That would get to anyone, dear. And now, with the actor taking his own life, who knows how Mr. Carraday will react to the news. But then it isn't really any of your concern, dear. Or mine, for that matter. I wouldn't worry if I were you. You're his employee, and this little tragedy shouldn't affect your job in the least."

"I..." Andrea suddenly felt like screaming at the waitress to stop. Poor Maggie. So eager to share the latest gossip, never suspecting the nightmarish effect it was having on her captive audience. "Would you bring me a cup of coffee, please, Maggie. I... guess I just need to eat something."

Maggie scooted out of the booth. "Why didn't you tell me? I'll get your coffee right away. Our lunch specials today are stuffed peppers and meat loaf with mashed potatoes and creamed corn. Which sounds good to you?"

Andrea's stomach gave a turn. "Maybe a bacon, lettuce, and tomato sandwich instead."

Maggie's eyebrows shot up. "Only that? Fries or coleslaw on the side? Or how about onion rings? We bread our own and cook 'em up fresh."

"No. Just the BLT, Maggie."

The waitress scurried off and returned with a steaming

mug, which she set in front of Andrea. "Oh, there was another piece of news, dear. Just heard about it yesterday. And this one's *good* news—at least for the town. It's helped boost Mr. Carraday's image another notch in the eyes of folks around here. Word is that he's just bought the cannery and intends to move a good share of his business to Seacliff. Gave a fair offer on the building, too—which means the cannery company can buy up the abandoned warehouse they've had their eye on, and that'll help our economy."

Maggie beamed. She bent in a motherly fashion over Andrea and touched her arm. "Now, dear, I want you to take care of yourself. Eat good, square meals and get your sleep. As long as Mr. Carraday's treating you with respect and you like your work, you should be able to make a decent wage out there. Never mind what I said about the house."

The best that Andrea could do was conjure a wan smile for Maggie. She drank her coffee quickly, nearly scalding her mouth. When the BLT arrived, she forced down as much of it as she could. Then she left the amount of the bill plus a generous tip by her plate and slipped out of the café before Maggie could trap her in more conversation.

Andrea headed for the beach instead of Ravenspire. She needed the fresh air, the scent of the ocean, the time and space to meditate and digest the news of Dane Clifton's suicide. She needed to decide how best to approach Holt with the truth about his wife's death.

She paced the length of the small shoreline and back several times, until finally her head cleared. She realized it was futile to try to figure out what was going through Dane's mind when he took his fatal plunge into the Pacific. But she did come to the conclusion that she must talk to Holt without delay and in as forthright a manner as possible.

She couldn't conceive how she would handle the agony of being in the same room with him, knowing that she would never again experience the pure pleasure of being held in his arms. How could she meet his eyes and bear the thought of leaving Ravenspire and the little girl who had captured her heart?

Trudging slowly to her car, she felt as if she were caught in the web of a senseless dream. She grasped at the one piece of news in which she'd found solace. Holt had bought the cannery and was moving his business to Seacliff. The act spoke volumes to Andrea. It told her that he was serious about making a commitment to spend more time with his daughter in the future. And if Maggie's perception was correct, he now had the sympathy of the villagers in his favor. Andrea suspected he cared little whether the locals hated him or loved him. But their newfound respect for him should benefit Elizabeth in the years to come, she reasoned, and in that hope she could find some small comfort.

Andrea spotted Holt's car through the trees as she came up the driveway of Ravenspire. The Lexus was parked near the front door. What she didn't see until she was almost upon it was the sheriff's cruiser that was parked at a haphazard angle a short distance ahead of the Lexus.

She drove on around to the garage and came in the rear entrance of the house. No sooner had she closed the back door than Sybil rushed out from the kitchen to meet her.

"This came for you, Miss," the cook said, shoving a white envelope into Andrea's hands. "A man in a uniform—a messenger, I reckon—came to the door, said this was to be delivered straight to you."

Andrea stared at the business-size envelope. The outside of it was blank. She thanked the cook, then started down the corridor.

"I hope it's not more bad news," Sybil called after her.

Glancing back, Andrea saw the dejected expression on Sybil's face. "I hope not, too," she said and went on.

Andrea stopped near the end of the long hall. She tore open the envelope. The sound of men's voices drifted from the foyer. She couldn't make out what they were saying, but she recognized the one voice as Holt's. The other, she assumed, belonged to the sheriff, and she imagined that the law officer had come to inform Holt of Dane Clifton's apparent suicide.

Andrea leaned against the wall and unfolded the single sheet of paper that was tucked in the envelope. Her hands began to tremble as she read the message:

Let it be known, Miss Lane, that it was your beauty and utter sincerity that trapped my cynical heart in the end. I can't let you go on believing a lie. The child is completely and legitimately Holt Carraday's and not mine—whatever coincidental resemblance there might be between the two of us. To my lasting regret, at the time of the child's conception, I was seeking comfort in the arms of a Swedish model at a cozy cottage in the Pennines. Don't grieve for me now, Miss Lane. I had six months more at best, according to my good doctor in London. I never could stand the thought of a slow, agonizing death. So you see, you were right. I am a coward at heart.

Andrea didn't know how long she stood there, rereading the hastily scrawled words. Vaguely, she realized that the conversation in the foyer was over. There was the sound of footsteps retreating down the west corridor. When their echo died away, Andrea went up to her rooms. Her face felt feverish, and she splashed cold water on her cheeks and brow. Then she put on fresh makeup and went in search of Holt.

She found him in the Grand Hall. He was staring out the window, backlit by the one lamp that was turned on in the huge room. Her throat constricted when she saw that he wore the same midnight black jacket, ivory sweater, and gray slacks he'd worn the day of her interview.

The instant she set foot in the room, he turned and began to walk toward her. When their gazes met, she thought that she had never seen him look more handsome—or more guarded.

Holt spoke first. "The sun's breaking through the clouds,"

he said, turning his face to the window. "The sky should clear before nightfall."

"I've been hoping to see the sun," she said. The yearning to be taken into his embrace burned inside her like the heat from a thousand suns. "How is your aunt?" she asked, amazed that her voice could sound so normal.

"Jayne will survive, but she'll need professional care the rest of her life. There's a facility near the hospital," he said quietly, "that came highly recommended to me by a business associate whose mother lives there. I've made arrangements for Jayne to be transferred to the home as soon as the doctor thinks it's advisable."

"You did all that you possibly could for her."

"I hope so," was his only response.

A deafening silence fell between them. Andrea sensed that she and Holt were walking an emotional tightrope. If either of them wavered from their charade of polite formality, the other was bound to follow—and that would make what she had to tell him even more difficult.

Finally, Holt strode to a table near the window and returned with a sheet of paper.

"You need to read this," he said, handing her the paper.

It was a letter addressed to the office of the sheriff in Seacliff. Andrea recognized the handwriting as Dane Clifton's.

The letter was nothing short of a confession. The actor wrote, in often vivid terms, of his relationship with Victoria and of the circumstances surrounding her accidental death. Toward the end, he mentioned "Miss Lane," whom he generously credited with prompting him to come forward. He didn't address his decision to take his own life, though he did conclude the lengthy letter by declaring that he could now go "into that endless night of sleep with my conscience clear at last."

"There was a note on the body," Holt said, "directing the authorities to a certain motel room, where they found the letter."

"I have something you should read, too." She passed him

the note. Swallowing a tear, she watched Holt's expression. A look of surprise registered on his face.

"I'd wondered." He folded the note and laid it aside with the letter. "Victoria had gone to Europe just before the time when Elizabeth was conceived. In my mind, there had always been a question of whether she and Clifton had resumed their affair. Then after Elizabeth's birth..."

Passing a hand over his face, Holt continued, "Victoria and I had what you'd call a whirlwind courtship. Clifton, for all his declarations that Victoria was the one great love of his life, had broken off with her to have a fling with a Spanish cabaret singer. On our honeymoon in Switzerland, Victoria suffered a miscarriage. Her pregnancy was in the very early stages."

Andrea drew in a sharp breath. "She was expecting Dane Clifton's child?" She no longer wondered why Holt had looked so grim at Jayne's mention of his honeymoon.

"I considered leaving her," he went on, "but I couldn't go through with it. Victoria was distraught and ill after the miscarriage, and by the time I'd brought her home to Ravenspire, I'd given up on the idea of a divorce." He met Andrea's gaze fully. "I want you to know," he said, "that I've always thought of Elizabeth as *my* daughter—whether she shared my genes or not."

"I do know," she assured him, dangerously close to confessing that she loved him.

Holt left her and strode toward the doors that led into the corridor. In a moment, when Andrea glanced up, she saw stars and a slice of silver moon on the darkened ceiling of the Grand Hall. With the same sense of awe that she'd experienced the first time she'd seen the light show, she watched Orion begin his journey across the winter sky.

"What will you do now?" Holt asked at her side.

No matter how tactfully they'd been couched, his cool words of dismissal dealt a blow to her heart.

"I've been thinking of contacting the academy. I was told when I left that I could return at any time. All I need to do is pick up the phone." She was proud of herself for sounding so rational when her heart was shattering into a million jagged pieces.

"You'll receive a fair amount of severance pay, of course, under the circumstances."

"I don't need special favors," she suddenly snapped.

"It isn't a favor," he returned sharply.

They fell silent again. Finally, she couldn't help asking, "What about you?"

"Doing something I've put off for too long. I've bought the old Seacliff cannery building and I'm moving the headquarters of my business here. There'll be time now for trips to Disney World," he said. A smile briefly animated his features. "And you'll be glad to know that John's started repairs on the rabbit hutches. The cages need to be in good shape if we're going to be raising rabbits again."

Andrea tried to return his smile, but her lower lip trembled. "I'd ... Excuse me. I have some things to do," she stammered. Blinking back tears, she couldn't resist a last glance at him. But his attention appeared to be on the ceiling.

What was I expecting? she thought. *To be swept into his arms and told that he can't bear to live without me?*

With as much dignity as she could summon, she began to walk away. She could almost hear Nanna admonish, *"Hold your head high, Andy. You've done what you set out to accomplish. Be proud. And move on with your life."*

"Don't go."

Andrea's footsteps faltered; she came to a stop just short of the corridor. Slowly, she turned toward Holt, fearful that her imagination had conjured up the plea that sounded as if it had been wrenched from his soul.

They stared at each other across the vastness of the Grand Hall. Then he held out his arms to her, and she fairly flew into his embrace. Holt pressed his face to her hair, rained kisses on her cheek, the scar, her ear. His hands burned a trail over her back as his lips ravished hers with sweet, intoxicating promises.

She pulled back to gaze into the fathomless depths of his eyes, and she knew she had been right, after all, to conclude there were no longer any barriers between them.

"Can you guess," she said, tracing the line of his jaw, "what I pictured when I got my first glimpse of this room?"

"What did you picture?"

"A fabulous party. I could see the couples dancing, hear their laughter and the enchanting strains of the orchestra. For a minute, I almost forgot why I was here."

"The Hall's seen its share of parties in the past. My grandmother's wedding reception was hosted here." He looked around. "Maybe it's time for another wedding ball. In fact, I think I hear the orchestra tuning up now. Do you hear it, too?" he said. "Do you hear the music, Andrea?"

"Yes," she whispered, "and it's beautiful."

Holt laughed softly, and she thought it was the loveliest melody of all.

Locked in each other's arms, they began to move in time to the music that only they could hear, while on the ceiling of the Grand Hall, Orion completed his journey across the winter sky.